BAD Guy — Rough Justice!

In pursuing the notorious Silver Dollar Gang, undercover agent Drew Henry is catapulted into a bizarre criminal conspiracy in the Wyoming town of Bridger. Three deputies have disappeared in mysterious circumstances, leading Drew to place himself in the firing line as the fourth potential victim. Suspicions abound as to the identity of the culprits. But only when he accidentally stumbles upon a robbery do the grim facts begin to emerge.

A break comes when an outlaw Drew thought had escaped the long arm of the law suddenly turns up. The outlaw's objective is to blackmail the perpetrators of the robbery scam with exposure. Drew must use all his skills as a BAD boy to bring all the guilty parties to justice. But this proves far more dangerous than he could ever have foreseen.

BAD Guy — Rough Justice!

Ethan Flagg

A Black Horse Western

ROBERT HALE

ISBN 978-0-7198-3061-7

The Crowood Press
The Stable Block
Crowood Lane
Ramsbury
Marlborough
Wiltshire SN8 2HR

www.bhwesterns.com

Robert Hale is an imprint
of The Crowood Press

Typeset by
Derek Doyle & Associates, Shaw Heath
Printed and bound in Great Britain by
4Bind Ltd, Stevenage, SG1 2XT

CHAPTER ONE

BAD MAN DOWN

'Hey, buddy,' Waxy Burnett called out to his partner. The two riders had drawn their horses to a halt beside a lone pine tree. A gloved finger pointed to a poster nailed to its trunk. 'Take a look at this.' The stark headline – *Wanted* – had caught the outlaw's attention, but more so the reward of a thousand bucks for the capture of the notorious Silver Dollar Gang. Burnett hawked out an indignant snort of derision. 'Is that all we're worth?'

His pard was equally scathing. 'The brainless saps must figure they're up against a much larger outfit.' The gurgling chuckle mocked the notion. 'I ain't never heard of a gang of two before.' His buddy's fervent nod of agreement endorsed the assertion.

The two owlhoots were as different as chalk and cheese. Burnett was a stout jasper of substantial girth, in stark contrast to the aptly named Skinny Jim

Fresno, who resembled a starved beanpole. For the past year the pair had robbed and killed their way across Colorado with impunity, giving no thought to the effect of their heinous rampaging.

Their repellent calling card was to leave a silver dollar in the mouth of each dead victim. The bizarre habit had quickly brought them to the attention of the authorities. But it was simple to evade capture with the law spread so thinly in the state's mountainous terrain. And with any pursuit concentrating on a substantial gang, the shrewd twosome had every reason to be smugly confident. As a result they were positively revelling in the notoriety their depredations had engendered.

So here they were, heading for the latest boom settlement where a substantial vein of gold had recently been uncovered. But the sight of this wanted dodger, which was no doubt splashed across the rest of the territory, had disturbed the recognized leader of the duo. Waxy had thus far given no thought to their vulnerability. He tried laughing it off. The pair had worked well as a team, each supporting the other.

Nevertheless Waxy's calculating brain began looking to maybe quit the scene for a spell, let the trail cool off. The portly jasper had mistakenly reckoned they had become untouchable, able to disappear into the vast expanse of Colorado's mountain country after each robbery.

Until now. This poster was now causing him some alarm, and he voiced his disquiet to Skinny Jim. 'Looks like the law could be closing in, pal,' he said, somewhat uneasily. 'What say we pull this one last job, then hightail it west to Brown's Park?' He studied his partner's thin features for his reaction to the suggestion. 'If'n we can fill our saddle bags with one big heist,' he pressed, 'it will be enough to set us up on easy street until the heat dies down.'

'Reckon you could be right, Waxy,' Fresno concurred. 'No sense in overdoing it.'

The Park was a notorious hideout for desperadoes on the run. No lawman had ever been able to penetrate this isolated enclave on the Utah/Wyoming border and live to tell the tale. It had been colonized by a certain Spanish missionary, Father Ortiz, back in 1650, but the Indians had burnt his settlements to the ground. Later, in the early nineteenth century, fur trappers arrived, and such famous names as Jim Bridger and Kit Carson established a lucrative trade with the Ute and Shoshone tribes. Not until after the Civil War did it become a favoured haven for outlaws, who lived side-by-side with legitimate settlers who provided a much needed refuge.

And so it was agreed. 'At least they haven't gotten a look at our handsome faces,' Waxy snorted nudging his horse northwards.

A couple of days later they crossed the Divide, heading down valley. Their aim was to follow the Laramie River to its junction with the Canadian, where news of the latest gold strike had sizzled down the grapevine. On their left the towering splendour of the Medicine Bow Range rose stark and majestic. Patches of snow still clung to the higher reaches, even in July. The weather was fine and bright, a clear azure sky heralding another hot day. But in this mountain country that could quickly change at the drop of a hat.

Fresno drew his horse to a halt. His brow furrowed, a finger pawing at his neck. 'That itch bothering you again, buddy?' his pard asked. Both men knew what the irritation meant. It was some form of innate hunch that danger was looming, a gut reaction that had saved their bacon on more than one occasion before.

'I've had this feeling since we crossed the Divide,' Fresno iterated, continuing to ease the prickliness. 'It must have been sparked by that wanted dodger.'

'You reckon we've gotten us a buzzard on our tail?' Waxy had always harboured a deep respect for his pal's uncanny knack of sniffing out unwanted predators. 'Must be some darned bounty hunter hoping to grab that reward.' Nervous peepers now scanned their back trail. Nothing moved.

'Reckon that must be what it is,' Fresno concurred. A jumpy tic made his left eye flicker as he also peered back down the trail. The assumed shadow was keeping well hidden. But there was no doubt in his mind that some unwanted irritant was back there.

'We'll keep going nice and steady and find us a good spot to ambush the critter,' Waxy declared, gently nudging his mount forwards. Ten minutes later they found the perfect place. Each man took up position on either side of the trail where it had been squeezed to single file by a stack of boulders on either side. And there they settled down, rifles pointing back along the trail. Ten minutes later the steady clip of hoofs assailed their acute hearing. And lo and behold, a rider hove into view.

An evil grin warped Burnett's leathery contours. He raised a thumb to his pal on the opposite side of the trail, then jabbed a finger at his chest. A nod from Fresno indicated he also had spotted the badge adorning the pursuer's vest.

At twenty yards out from the gap, two rifles blasted apart the silence. The bushwhacked rider stood no chance. He was punched back off his horse. And there he lay, still and lifeless. The killers waited a moment before gingerly approaching the still form. Waxy toed the body. No need for another bullet. The lawdog was dead as a graveyard. The badge was ripped from the dead man's chest. Waxy spat on it. 'Damn blasted BAD agent!' was the snarled exclamation. 'With them guys on the prod, it sure is time for a long vacation in Brown's Park.'

Fresno aimed a vicious boot into the lifeless corpse before stuffing their macabre calling card in the open mouth. The owlhooters then mounted up and continued on their way.

CHAPTER TWO

NO JOY IN PARADISE

It was not until later the following day that they arrived on the edge of a shabby huddle of buildings. Hats were pulled low, as much to conceal their stubble-coated faces as shade out the setting sun. Since their encounter with the BAD – Bureau of Advanced Detection – agent, both men had maintained a sharp lookout for other unwelcome predators. Thankfully no more itching had occurred.

A roughly painted signboard told them they were about to enter the town of Paradise: elevation 5,746 feet. The population of 589 had recently been crossed out and amended to 587. Burnett spat out a mocking guffaw. 'I wonder what happened to those two?' he mused.

His buddy offered a sardonic wisecrack with an apathetic shrug. 'Just so long as they weren't caught muscling in on our job, who cares?'

Waxy couldn't help but agree, while checking his pistol was fully loaded. 'Paradise!' he snorted, aiming a glob of spittle at the sign. 'That's a joke if ever there was one.'

A critical eye was cast over the untidy array of mean structures and tents that appeared to have been thrown up with little consideration to any kind of organized planning. Such was the genesis of a boom town in the making where gold was the principal reason for its inception. And when that had been completely removed, the place would be left to rot as prospectors moved on to the next strike.

A stubby finger pointed skywards. 'Looks like a storm's brewing up,' Fresno commented. Already dark clouds were bunching to the east, girding themselves in readiness for the coming onslaught. Neither outlaw minded that at all. Indeed it was an advantage. Moments later the first droplets bounced off their hats.

'This should be a piece of cake,' Burnett jeered. 'Once the clouds break we'll have the street to ourselves. No chance of anybody sticking a beaky snout where it ain't wanted.'

Within minutes the bubbling ferment overhead had gobbled up the yellow orb of the sun. The two men quickly donned their waterproof ponchos just before the heavens opened. Casually walking their horses down the main street, folks could be seen quickly disappearing under cover to avoid a drenching. Nobody paid any heed to the newcomers. Two

11

pairs of hawkish eyes panned either side of the street, probing the huddle of ugly buildings for the one they sought.

Tension was mounting, backs stiffening as they approached the outskirts. But there it was, and a double sigh of relief hissed from between gritted teeth. Well placed, too. Ideal for a quick getaway. Flashes of lightning forked across the darkening sky, crackling like fiery twigs. Less than a minute passed before the ominous rumble of thunder akin to some cosmic drum roll shook the ground. A chilling precursor to the task about to be enacted.

Being a double act meant they could not tackle the bigger heists. Smaller jobs netted less, but they had discovered early on that assay offices were the most lucrative, inevitably holding substantial amounts of paper money to feed the miners' insatiable scramble to cash in their paydirt. In the more remote areas, gold itself was the prime currency, and this had led to them waylaying lone prospectors carrying their poke to the nearest town.

After a quick look round to ensure they were not being observed, the two brigands tied up their mounts outside the small office. A light burning inside told them the agent was still innocently beavering away. Waxy looked at his buddy, and a tight nod passed between them. This had been done many times before, so they each knew what to do.

Waxy peered through the grimy window offering a leer of satisfaction when he saw the agent weighing gold dust and noting down the various tallies in a ledger. Sepia photographs of successful miners covered the plank walls of the small room. Also reflected in the dim glow were the trappings of their profession: picks, shovels and sifting pans.

Guns gripped tight, the two bandits pushed open the door and stepped inside. 'Raise your mitts, fella,' Burnett snapped wafting the gun in the startled clerk's face. 'This is a heist. Make a sound and you're a dead man. Savvy?' The terrified clerk nodded. His shaking hands grabbed for the roof. Satisfied there would be no retaliation from this scared rabbit, Burnett's eyes glittered at the sight of the yellow peril. 'Now open that safe and stuff those greenbacks in this sack.' He tossed an empty flour bag onto the counter. The man just stood there, frozen to the spot. Waxy jabbed the gun in his ribs. 'Shift your ass, mister,' he snapped. 'We ain't got all day. And no tricks, or this beauty spits hot lead.'

Meanwhile, Fresno was keeping watch on the street outside. They only bothered with lifting the heavier raw material if paper currency was in short supply. With the bag filled, Waxy declared, 'You came good, mister. So we'll say goodbye, and much obliged.' He shook his head in a pseudo apology. 'Pity you've seen our handsome faces though. There's only one answer to that.' He nodded to his partner. 'Your turn this time, Skinny.'

Fresno's angular kisser broke into a lurid grin. 'This is the part I like. And just at the right time.' His fiery gaze lifted towards the roof. A blast of thunder overhead effectively masked that of the bucking six

13

gun. An orange tongue of flame erupted from the barrel. The clerk stood no chance, and he went down in a heap behind the counter. 'Time we hightailed it,' he whooped. 'Let's go!' The corpulent bandit paused to stuff their bizarre fixation in the dead man's mouth.

Then without checking his condition, they rushed outside and mounted up. The growling from above rumbled on as they left Paradise, with nobody any the wiser as to the grisly deed that had just been performed. 'Well, buddy, that's one more jasper to remove from this dump's population tally.' Shrieks of manic laughter were whipped away by the howling gale as they disappeared, swallowed up by the storm.

As with most guys who follow the outlaw trail, the presence of easy dough was too much of a temptation to resist. The adage that encourages an attitude of easy come, easy go becomes impossible to ignore. All those lovely greenbacks were burning a hole in their pockets. After crossing the mountains at Zirkel Pass, they dropped down to accompany the infant Snake River to reach the Wyoming border town of Bear Claw six days after leaving Paradise.

There they booked into the best hotel and immediately began living the high life, ostensibly as gold prospectors who had struck it rich. Wine, women and song, not necessarily in that order, vied to gobble up the greenbacks alongside the compulsion to gamble. Three weeks later the inevitable happened: they ran out of funds.

Unable to pay the extensive hotel bill, they were

forced to flee in the middle of the night with barely enough money left to buy trail grub from the next trading post. 'What we gonna do now, Waxy?' Skinny Jim groaned. 'Ain't no chance of us living it up in Brown's Park with empty pockets.'

The answer to their dilemma arrived by accident, a fortuitous meeting between the devious pair and a travelling prospector. They were camped in a hollow beside a creek in the shadow of Big Pinny Mountain a few miles east of the Divide. Both men were morosely grumbling about their poverty-stricken lot when a call came from the edge of the clearing.

'Hullo the camp,' a gravelly voice called out. 'Friendly traveller coming in.' It was the obligatory greeting by new arrivals to avoid a hot reception from nervous six-shooters. A dishevelled old timer emerged from the gloom, leading a burro loaded up with mining gear. 'Any chance of some vittles for a hungry jasper, boys?'

The sight of the prospecting accoutrements immediately kindled the interest of the two campers. 'Sure thing, mister. Come on in and welcome,' a rejuvenated Waxy Burnett declared, pasting an oily smile on his jowly kisser. 'We ain't gotten much to offer, just a bit of scrawny rabbit and some refried beans. But at least the coffee's hot and strong.'

'The name's Sluice Mulligan,' the man offered, readily accepting a burnt leg sitting on a plate of unwholesome mush. 'I've been on the trail for three days. My grub ran out yesterday. Spotting your camp sure was a stroke of luck. I didn't fancy providing a meal for some greedy coyote. Not that there'd be much for the scavenging critter to gnaw on.' Sluice chuckled at his own joke, as he ravenously shovelled down the grub.

'Pity we ain't gotten any bacon to perk up that goo,' Fresno added, joining in with a strained laugh, struggling to preserve an air of hospitality. All the while the eyes of both men kept flitting towards the heavily laden burro.

'This'll do fine, boys,' the old-timer breezed, his attention focused on filling his belly. 'I'm much obliged for the kindly welcome into your camp.'

'So where you headed, Sluice?' Waxy enquired, trying not to sound too nosey. 'This is mighty rough country for a guy to be travelling on his ownsome.'

The flickering light from the camp fire reflected a gleam of triumph in the old jigger's rheumy peepers. He reached into his pocket and drew out a single gold nugget and held it up. Like many such jaspers who have struck it rich, the guy could not keep his mouth shut.

'Take a look at that, boys,' he warbled, holding up the glittering chunk in a grubby paw. The two watchers gazed in fascinated wonder at the dazzling prize, mouths gaping wide. Energized by the mesmerizing effect the eye-opener was having on his audience, Sluice launched into how he had come by the life-changing find. 'And there's a heap more where that came from. I'm headed for Baggs to register my claim.'

While the old prospector was innocently babbling

on about his discovery in a remote cleft boasting the hauntingly appropriate name of Broken Wheel Gulch, surreptitious looks were passing between the sneaky outlaws. Fresno casually stood up and announced, 'I'll just get some more wood for the fire.' Sluice didn't even notice, so raptly was he describing his good fortune. Once out of the firelight, Fresno circled around behind his victim. The large bandanna was uncoiled from around his neck and rolled into a tight flex.

Teeth gleamed in a feral grin as he slowly crept up behind the unsuspecting dupe. Burnett made sure to keep the old guy's attention. For a brief moment time ceased to exist. A flitting instant betwixt life and death. The garrotte lifted in slow motion, held tightly in both hands. Then a flick over the guy's head, a sharp tug, and life was being choked from the poor sucker. Fresno squeezed hard, desperately trying to strangle his victim.

Waxy urged his pard to greater effort. 'Pull it tighter,' he yelled. 'It can't be that hard to throttle the old buzzard.' But the grisly task was proving far more of a struggle than he had imagined. Sluice Mulligan was one resilient cookie. Kicking and writhing for all he was worth, his gnarled fingers strove to release the pressure on his neck.

Waxy could see that his partner's grip was weakening. He drew his revolver. The hammer snapped back ready to deliver the killing shot. But the noise of gunfire this close to the main trail might attract unwelcome attention. Waxy cursed. It would have to be cold steel. Without any further hesitation, he drew a ten-inch Bowie knife from the sheath on his belt and plunged it into the old boy's scraggy chest. Once, twice it slid effortlessly between the bony ribs.

The struggling immediately ceased. The contest was over. Sluice Mulligan had suffered the fatal consequences of his inability to keep quiet. The killers lay down flat on the ground, sweat pouring from their ashen faces. 'Jeepers, buddy!' Fresno exclaimed sucking in huge lungfuls of air. 'I never reckoned that would be so hard.'

'You ain't wrong there, pal,' Waxy gasped. 'That guy was one tough old Charlie!'

After recovering their breath, and helped by the final slugs from a whiskey bottle, they made a thorough search of the dead man's possessions. A sack containing gold nuggets, flakes and dust was laid out on the ground. For upwards of ten minute the thieves stared at their ill-gotten gains. It was Waxy who broke the heavy silence. 'This lot will sure set us up for a tidy spell in Brown's Park.'

'And this time, we won't stop off any place and lose it at the tables,' added a thoughtful Skinny Jim Fresno.

It was too late in the day for continuing their journey west, so the merciless duo shifted their dead companion away from the camp, propping him up against a tree. The mandatory silver dollar, their last one, was stuck in his mouth. 'Nobody can say we don't pay our way,' Waxy declared with a macabre grin. 'Although you were a mite reluctant

18

until I persuaded you otherwise, Sluice.' They both sniggered uproariously at their gallows humour.

Sleep came easy to the cold-hearted killers that night. A smouldering fire kept the predators at bay as the callous duo dreamed of continuing the party interrupted in Bear Claw. Next morning they were soon on the trail, having relieved the dead prospector of his worthy poke. Both men tipped their hats to the sitting body as they passed. 'Much obliged for your generosity, old-timer,' Waxy scoffed.

'And we'll make sure to spend it wisely,' added Fresno. Macabre chuckles echoed around the abandoned death site. A wandering hawk cawed overhead, greedily surveying an effortless meal ticket. Not the slightest inkling passed across the warped minds of the notorious Silver Dollar Gang that they had become the focal point of an organization dedicated to the eradication of their heinous marauding.

CHAPTER THREE

BAD MAN'S JUSTICE

Drew Henry was feeding the hens when his brother-in-law arrived at the ranch. And judging by the steam rising from his mount's flanks, not to mention the stern look that had taken over Sam Vender's normally genial expression, he had not ridden over merely to chew the cud. A frown of concern creased Drew's craggy face. Sam had been made sheriff of Rock Springs, Wyoming, following the break-up of the infamous Vender Gang led by his lawless brother Cain the previous year.

As an undercover agent for the Bureau of Advanced Detection, a secretive law enforcement agency more commonly known as BAD, Drew was instrumental in bringing the culprits to justice, one of whom had been the dishonest Sheriff Tash Speakman.*

Drew nodded to his kinsman but said nothing, waiting for him to get his breath and deliver his message that was clearly nothing to do with the current price of eggs. 'A letter arrived this morning from Laramie and I figured you would want to have it straightaway,' the lawman blurted out. 'It must be important for a pony express courier to deliver it.' The heading on the envelope depicted two crossed revolvers surmounted by a bald eagle – a clear sign to the retired BAD boy that his unique talents were once again being requested.

Drew held the missive in his hands for a moment. 'Ain't you gonna open it?' enquired the impatient lawman, curious as to the contents of a letter depicting such a strange emblem. No mention had been made by Drew regarding the secret organization for whom he had worked during the period spent breaking up the shameful depredations caused by the lawless Vender kin. Of the family, only Sam and his sister Ruth had remained immune from their brothers' heinous activities.

Following a brief courtship after the much reported trial held in Rock Springs, Ruth and Drew had married. The six months of wedlock before she succumbed to a sudden attack of prairie fever had

*This is the third adventure involving the BAD Agency. The others can be experienced in *Outlaw Queen* and *Send for the BAD Guy!,* Black Horse Westerns from Crowood also written by Ethan Flagg.

been the happiest of Drew's life, and her sudden death had left him bereft of the will to live. It was Sam and his new deputy Angus McVay who had restored his faith in himself, and thereafter he had thrown himself into keeping the ranch going. Now the spread could be regarded as a successful enterprise.

Drew had no wish for that to be disrupted by another assignment from the BAD organization. But this was easier said than done. He continued to stare at the unopened letter, knowing what it contained. Much as he would have preferred to ignore the missive, he knew in his heart that this was impossible. And no matter how much he might try denying it, the lure of excitement, the thrill of pitting his wits against ruthless desperadoes, was eating away at his resolve. Had Ruth still been alive, he would most assuredly have snubbed the summons.

Ranching was satisfying enough in its own way, but with his beloved wife gone, things could never be the same again. It was now much easier to admit the truth that nothing quite matched the pursuit of villains, and playing a key role in establishing the rule of law and order across the wild frontier territories. 'Are we gonna stand here all day, Drew?' Sam pressured him, making little attempt to hide his curiosity. 'A reply might be needed.'

The abrupt interruption to his churning thoughts brought Drew back to the present. Slowly he slit open the envelope and removed the letter. 'Just as I thought,' he muttered to himself. 'Another summons from the director.' The quizzical look from his brother-in-law led Drew finally to concede in revealing his double life to the stunned lawman. 'You've heard about the BAD organization?' A hesitant nod found him continuing: 'Well, it was the killing of my brother Cole that brought me to these parts. He was one of their field operators, same as me. That's how I came to be involved with bringing your brothers to justice.'

After reading the letter, as expected his presence was respectfully requested at the Bureau's headquarters in Laramie as soon as possible. It was signed by Theophilus Wainwright, Field Director of Operations. No mention of the job to be undertaken was mentioned, doubtless for security reasons.

'Thunderation! A secret agent. Who could have guessed it?' Sam exclaimed, trying to come to terms with his friend's hidden life. 'You sure kept that quiet. So do you want me to post a reply telling them that you'll go?'

'I kept it secret for Ruth's sake,' Drew made clear. 'There are too many bandits out there who'd rather have BAD boys like me pushing up the daisies. I couldn't take that chance. But there ain't no riding around the fact that working for the Bureau gets into a man's blood. It's something you can't just throw off like an old coat. So the answer to your query is – yes, I am going. Cash Scarborough, my foreman, can look after things around here while I'm away. But I'll deliver the reply personally. It'll be a sight quicker than the overland mail.'

Already Drew's thoughts were pondering on what the Bureau wanted his unique talents for this time. There were no more kinfolks to meet a grisly end. So it had to be something really critical for him to be urgently summoned like this.

A week's hard riding found Drew Henry entering the BAD office on Cheyenne Boulevard in Laramie. Even though some considerable time had elapsed since he had been here previously, the place didn't appear to have changed one jot. But then he remembered: of course it had. The nameplate on the door to the main office was a stark reminder of the hazardous nature of the Bureau's clandestine work. His old boss, Isaac Thruxton, had been shot dead by Cain Vender during the attempted train hold-up at Table Rock, and another man was now ensconced behind the same desk. His name was Theophilus Wainwright.

'Glad you could make it, Drew,' the man said, standing up and holding out a hand of welcome. 'The Bureau is in desperate need of your assistance.'

Drew looked the man over, accepting the greeting with a wary nod. Wainwright's grip was as hard as the serious look filtering from eyes of deepest blue. 'I'm wondering whether this is going to be an agreeable meeting or not, sir,' he confessed, giving him a quizzical look to acknowledge his uncertainty.

Well dressed in a midnight blue suit, the director was around the sixty mark, with thick, iron-grey hair complementing the moustache gracing his upper lip. Drew had never previously come into contact with the guy, but everybody in the Bureau knew he had been a renowned and highly successful man hunter himself before rising to his current position. 'I know that you and Isaac held each other in the highest regard,' Wainwright averred, noting his visitor's restrained puzzlement. 'I can only hope that I live up to the high expectations that he fostered.' Hesitation, palpable and heavy, conveyed a sense of trepidation to the listener.

'So what is it you want from me, Mister Wainwright?' Drew asked, quietly but firmly.

The older man sat down, indicating for his visitor to do likewise. Now it was time to get down to business. Wainwright steepled his fingers, wondering how best to broach the problem for which he needed the BAD boy's unique assistance. 'We're being plagued by a band of killers known as the Silver Dollar Gang,' he declared, and launched into a description of the heinous depredations carried out over the last year. Clarification of the reason behind the name caused even a hardened agent like Drew Henry to feel the cold hand of the Grim Reaper crawling down his spine. 'Unlike many outlaw bands, these skunks have exhibited not the slightest hesitation in killing their victims, leaving no witnesses to their odious crimes.' He went on to outline the gang's ruthless exploits.

Drew's face hardened. From what the director had depicted, these were an evil bunch, to be sure. 'And you say they've left no clues as to their identities or whereabouts, merely disappearing into thin air?' Drew enquired, still uncertain as to why his presence was needed here. A crisp nod saw him adding: 'So I'll repeat the question. Why me? You still have plenty of good men equal to this task.'

Once again the director's response communicated a tight-lipped awkwardness. A hand slowly indicated the wall behind him. Drew's eyes shifted to the array of sepia photographs showing agents past and present. He couldn't help noting the increase in the number of black ribbons encompassing those who had died in the line of duty. Still his look was one of perplexity. Wainwright relieved his troubled frown by pointing a trembling finger at the burly agent whose black attire matched that of a waxed moustache. 'Take a closer look at the one on the end.'

That was when the penny dropped, and Drew's mouth hung open as the grim truth struck home like the kick from a loco mule: Ivory Jack Canton, his one-time partner and best friend . . . dead! He could barely credit what he was seeing. 'And it's this bunch of killers that have done for him,' Wainwright softly declared. 'I figured that if'n any of our men should track the varmints down, you should be given first call.'

Drew needed a moment to compose himself before responding. 'You did right, sir. But it's going to be a tough job not having anything to go on.'

'That would have been the case two weeks ago.' Wainwright had become much more enthused, now he knew that his summons had encouraged the desired effect. 'But they made a big mistake on their last robbery because the assay agent at Paradise in Colorado lived long enough to describe his assailants. And it turns out there are only two of the bastards!' The harsh expletive was spat out with venom. 'I've had a pen artist knock together a couple of portraits to go with the reward poster, which we've raised to two thousand dollars.'

Drew studied the drawings closely in silence, teeth clenched tight in fury as he stuffed the dodger into his pocket. So it was only a two-man gang he was after. 'These jaspers have to be mighty sharp-witted to cause all this mayhem. And to take down Ivory Jack in the process.' He allowed his intense anger to subside before snapping out: 'The scumbags have sealed their fate by making it a personal issue. And that's a promise. Give me the badge of office and swear me in.'

'There's one other clue we have to their where-abouts,' Wainwright stated, having performed the official ceremony with gusto. 'They took down a lone prospector only last week in a narrow gulch off the Canadian River this side of the Divide.'

Drew immediately caught the director's drift. 'That means they're headed in the direction of Brown's Park.' By this time the BAD boy was thoroughly in tune with his new assignment, and eager to get started. 'Once they reach the Flaming Gorge country, I won't stand a durned chance of winkling them out.'

'I agree. Best if'n you leave right away. Cut across

27

the Carbon Strip and you could cut them off at Bridger,' Wainwright asserted, also keen for the chase to commence forthwith. 'I'll give you a warrant to sign out a fast horse and whatever else you need from the Bureau's storage depot down town.'

Drew gave a curt nod. Pinning on the revered badge, he leapt to his feet. They shook hands, a tacit accord passing between them. Both men were fully aware of the dangers involved in such a hazardous mission. There might be only two of the critters, but they were cold-blooded in the extreme. He was heading out the door when the director's final comment rang in his ears: 'Bring those guys in Drew, over a saddle if'n necessary, and the reward money is all your'n.'

A flat look of disdain greeted the remark. 'I ain't doing this for the money, boss. Jack was a good friend of mine, one of the best, and he needs justice, along with all the other poor suckers whose lives these rats have terminated.'

CHAPTER FOUR

SHIVERING SNAKES!

Within the hour, Drew Henry was riding out of Laramie, saddle bags packed with all the essentials needed by men of his profession. The most careful acquisition had been a horse that combined both strength and stamina coupled with a sharp intelligence. The Indian-bred Barbary was ideal for catching up with his quarry.

Drew's intention was to ride fast and light. All agents were trained in the skill of living off the land – indeed, it was a friendly Arapaho brave who had been in charge of this most vital of training courses. And it was he who had suggested the Barbary as the finest of tracking mounts. As such, Drew was confident of being able to run these Silver Dollar brigands to earth.

As advised by Theophilus Wainwright, he headed west of north along the Medicine Bow valley, circling round the scalloped moulding of Elk Mountain to avoid having to cross the mountains by way of Snowy Range Pass. It was a longer route, but would save time. Thereafter he reached the southern limits of the Great Divide Basin known as the Carbon Strip. A vast, rolling grass-covered plain stretched before him.

He was travelling light to make good time so needed to live off the bounties that nature provided. This was a land of gentle rises and falls interspersed with stands of dwarf trees. Herds of antelope roamed freely, offering the lone traveller a source of their much favoured venison meat to offset regular trail fodder.

In the far distance, rising through a bank of haze, were the Rocky Mountains. Drew prayed that he would catch up with his quarry before they were able to cross this forbidding barrier. The border town of Bridger lay in the eastern shadow of the towering landmass. Before that another formidable barrier known as the Steamboat Wilderness had to be traversed.

On his third day on the trail, Drew stopped for the night at the Shivering Bear trading post. A remote enclave tucked under a rocky overhang for protection from the elements, it was run by a half-breed Shoshone called Joseph Yellow Knife. Many of these remote stations dotted the outback, providing much needed sustenance for weary travellers. Shivering

Bear was no different from the rest, a single-storey cluster of buildings made from stacked logs caulked with mud, the whole covered with wooden shingles.

On enquiring after the strange name of the post, Drew was informed that the intense winter cold often drove grizzly bears to seek shelter in its barn. 'They don't cause us any harm,' the proprietor explained, in that deep staccato redolent of his tribe as he poured his visitor a shot of rye whiskey, 'just so long as you leave them alone. Trying to waken a hibernating bear can be a dangerous chore,' the Indian added. When Drew slapped a coin down on the counter, Yellow Knife raised a hand: 'First drink on the house!'

A nod of appreciation found the newcomer amenably concluding that along with his squaw wife, this guy ran a tight ship. He was later able to confirm that positive view following a tasty meal made from natural products available in the region. In this respect Indians were past masters – and it avoided expensive mercantile supplies having to be brought in from distant towns.

While eating the antelope stew, his mind was mulling over the vital titbit of information passed on by Yellow Knife. Two hard-nosed characters had passed through the post three days before, and their description tallied with that of the wounded assay agent who had been left for dead back in Paradise. From what the breed had said, they appeared easygoing, and had even let slip their ultimate destination – Brown's Park. Drew knew then that he

31

was on the right trail, but he would have to push the Barbary hard in order to overtake the brigands before they reached Bridger.

So engrossed was he in enjoying the food and considering his future strategy, Drew failed to heed a man approaching to his rear. Only when a hand came to rest on his left shoulder was the natural instinct for survival triggered. Silently cursing his inept lack of attention, the agent quickly recovered. He grabbed hold of the alien intrusion and jerked the owner off balance. In the time it takes to say BAD boy, the unfortunate target was on the floor with a gun barrel jammed into his head.

Only then did the agent recognize his one-time deputy from Rock Springs. 'What in blue blazes are you doing, Angus?' he exclaimed, helping the young man to his feet. 'Coming up behind a guy like that! Didn't you learn anything back there? You could have gotten yourself killed!'

Thoroughly shaken up, Angus McVay stuttered out a hurried apology. 'Gee! I s-sure am s-sorry about that, Drew. It was such a surprise for me as well, coming across you in this remote outpost!'

The two men had been instrumental in quelling a potential lynch mob in Rock Springs when Sam Vender, the current sheriff, had been accused of being in cahoots with his thieving brothers. The deputy sheriff's badge pinned to his vest indicated that Angus was still in the job. Mystification as to the young man's presence registered on Drew's craggy face. 'This part of the territory is way outside your jurisdiction, boy. So what you doing down here?'

'Sam told me you had been called back to Laramie by your once employer,' Angus explained, accepting a cup of coffee and a smoke from his former mentor. 'On the same day, I received notification that I'd been accepted as a full time deputy sheriff in Bridger. So that's where I'm headed now.'

'That sure is good news, Angus. You deserve it,' Drew complimented the young man. 'I'm headed the same way. Perhaps we could join up. I'm tracking some bad guys calling themselves the Silver Dollar Gang. It would be good training for you.'

'I've heard tell about them,' Angus enthused excitedly. 'Evil skunks that leave a coin in the mouths of their victims. Running them down would sure be a feather in my cap when I reach Bridger.' Though his eagerness waned somewhat when he considered that a large gang could be more than two jaspers could handle.

Drew read the hesitation in his young colleague's anxious look. 'Don't worry, boy. This so-called gang only has two members. That said, they've caused a heap of mayhem, and are ruthless predators who ain't about to surrender without a fight. You up for that, Angus?'

'I sure am,' the young deputy gushed, displaying ardent zeal. 'You can count on me to back your play.'

Having been at the trading post since the previous evening, Angus was eager to hit the trail. 'You go make sure our horses are well fed and watered while I finish up this lip-smacking chow,' Drew said, stifling a yawn as he forked in a mouthful of the delicious stew. 'I can sleep in the saddle while you keep watch as we ride.'

A half hour later they bade farewell to Joseph Yellow Knife and his woman, and were picking their way up a steepening trail between tight-packed ranks of pine and spruce. Chipmunks, squirrels and cotton-tailed rabbits, initially curious to witness these strange intruders, soon scampered out of their path. The warm air of the valley soon became more chilled as height was gained, persuading the riders to don their fleece jackets.

Such was the isolation and inaccessibility of the rough terrain they needed to traverse that any sign left by previous travellers was of great interest. Especially if it indicated that only two horses had passed that way. Drew kept his eyes peeled. Trails were non-existent here in the Elkhorn Range, and navigation was only possible by tracking the sun's course across the sky. Luckily, Drew had his army compass to help them maintain a fairly accurate course.

Two days after leaving the Shivering Bear, his vigilance was rewarded. He pulled up. 'See that?' he said, pointing to a set of hoofprints. 'Looks like two riders passed this way. And not long since, judging by how clear the imprints are.' The trail had crossed a shallow creek, and it was on the far side that the obvious prints had been left embedded in the muddy bank.

'You reckon this could be them?' Angus asked with vigour. He was chafing at the bit, eager to catch up with the crooks and prove his worth to the more experienced agent.

'Ain't no reason to suppose otherwise,' Drew concurred. 'My guess is they're only a half-day's ride ahead – and they're not bothered about leaving a trail, neither. The clowns must figure they're safe from any pursuit out here in the wilds.' He maintained a level, even tone to temper his young companion's ardour. 'We'll need to keep watchful and fully alert from here on.'

The following day they had crested a rise and were about to descend a loose bank of scree when Angus pointed to a blue-grey coil of smoke snaking up from amidst the dense tract of tree-cloaked scrubland below. 'That has to be them!' he said breezily, all set to go in bold as you please.

Drew kept him on a tight rein. 'Slow and easy does it down this slope,' he cautioned. 'We don't want to issue a warning that they've gotten unwelcome company.' With infinite care they descended the tricky gradient, trying to avoid a trickle of loose stones becoming a landslide. By keeping to the firmer left-hand edge, they successfully negotiated the awkward descent. 'We'll split up and come at them from two sides,' Drew instructed his partner. 'You circle around to the right, and I'll go this way.'

The two men dismounted, ensuring their handguns were fully loaded before leading their mounts in a pincer movement. It was a military tactic that

35

Drew had perfected while a humble lieutenant in the 51st Ohio Infantry during the Civil War. Silent as a shadow he led the Barbary through the tight scattering of thickets. When he calculated that the hidden camp was close by, the faithful horse was tethered to a tree. 'We don't want those crafty buzzards knowing their goose has been cooked, do we old fella?' he said quietly into the horse's ear. Gun held tightly in his right hand, he made to move off.

'Too late for that, mister,' a guttural rasp snarled from behind. 'Your bird has already been burnt to a crisp. Now raise those mitts and keep still as the grave. There's a forty-five pointed right at your back.' The click of a hammer racking back proved this was no idle threat. Drew stiffened and did as directed. A silent curse was stifled. He had sadly underestimated the acuity of his foe. 'Now shuck that gun and move forward slowly,' the hidden voice ordered.

Unarmed and helpless, Drew was now at the mercy of those he had been tracking. How could he have been so foolish as to underrate the scheming duplicity of these brigands? But it was too late for recriminations now. He could only hope that Angus McVay was close by and would be capable of turning the tables.

As it happened, Skinny Jim Fresno's unexpected sighting of the tracker had occurred by pure accident. The pair of outlaws had been preparing a meal while mulling over their forthcoming vacation in Brown's Park. 'We need to rest up awhile here, Waxy,' the scrawny crook had asserted, picking up

36

the empty coffee pot. 'These nags are plumb tuckered out. I don't reckon mine will make it.'

Waxy nodded his agreement. 'Guess you're right there, Jim. Next settlement we come across, we can exchange them for decent mounts.' An ugly smirk soured his warped features. 'And anybody fool enough to object will get a taste of this.' He hauled out his six-gun and kissed the barrel. 'Nobody's gonna pick up our trail in these parts.' He then continued, stirring up the concoction of beans and chipmunk meat in a pan. 'You go fill up that pot at the creek so we can boil some fresh coffee.'

And that was it. Fresno had just happened to spot the shadowy form sneaking through the undergrowth, and had suspected the obvious. 'Now start walking!' the outlaw snapped harshly. 'And don't try no fancy tricks. My trigger finger is kinda twitchy!'

The captive had little choice but to obey. When they entered the camp some minutes later, Burnett leapt to his feet. 'So what have we here, Skinny? Some nosey critter figuring to bum a free meal?' That was when he received a shock as startling as that of his unwelcome visitor – and this one was especially galling to the stocky killer. 'Drew Henry!' he gasped out, momentarily lost for words, just like his opposite number. Both men stared open mouthed at each other. But having the upper hand, it was Burnett who recovered first. 'So what's a BAD boy like you doing sneaking up on innocent travellers out here in the wilds?' The question was issued in a mocking chortle. 'Lost your way?'

'You know this jasper, Waxy?' enquired a non-plussed Jim Fresno.

The ugly smile slipped from Burnett's face to be replaced with a hard leer of loathing. 'This darned skunk put me away for a ten spell in jail. And all on account of me trying to earn a decent living.' The follow-up comment was for his partner. 'That was before you and me teamed up.'

Now it was Drew's turn to recover his wits. He hawked out a derisory snort. 'Robbing innocent travellers ain't what either me or the court figured was an honest living. So how come you're out in three?'

A burst of hilarity rippled around the enclosed glade. 'No hoosegow in the whole goddamned country is gonna keep Waxy Burnett holed up for long. So I busted out when the guards weren't looking. Easy as pie. Then I headed north to escape the heat.' He then turned his attention back to the unlucky prisoner. 'And now you've fallen into my hands. That sure is providence smiling down on my head. And just in time for me to feed you to the wolves.' He rubbed his hands with glee. 'I've been praying for this moment ever since your blamed court sent me down to rot in that damn hell hole.'

His gun rose, the hammer cranking back. Slowly and with malicious pleasure Waxy Burnett took aim. 'Anything you want to say, BAD boy, afore my friend here calls time?'

'Guess you've gotten me hog-tied and corralled, Waxy.' Drew's voice had risen a notch, ostensibly displaying his fear, but in truth praying that his own pard would be alerted to the unholy plight he was now facing. 'But the law will catch up with you soon. And then there'll be a noose with your name on it.'

'Enough of this baloney, just shoot the damn critter, Waxy,' an impatient Fresno demanded. 'He's gotten a good horse back there, and I'm itching to reach Brown's Park.'

Eyes like hard chips of coal informed Drew that his time was fast ebbing away. And there wasn't a darned thing he could do about it. There was no sign of Angus McVay. Maybe the kid had gotten himself lost. It didn't matter now, anyway.

Having given up all hope of surviving the imminent gundown, a crackle of dried twigs at the edge of the clearing caught their attention. 'Drop those hoglegs and reach.' Burnett whirled about to face the unexpected threat. Drew's sigh of relief at his partner's intervention was cut short by the outlaw's gun panning round to blast the intruder. But Angus was ready for the move, and his own gun barked loud and accurate, the slug taking the owlhooter in the shoulder.

Burnett went down, out of the reckoning. But Skinny Jim now took over, his Cooper Navy spitting out an orange tongue of flame. It was meant as a killing shot, but the bullet struck Angus's pistol, and the weapon spun away. Drew took advantage of the mêlée to launch himself at the lean brigand, and before Fresno could deliver another shot, a solid hammer blow connected with the stubble-coated jaw, knocking Fresno to the ground.

Yet still the battle was not over. Although Burnett was badly wounded, he still had enough strength to raise his .45 Frontier. All set to let fly, Drew called out a warning: 'Look out, Angus!' The younger man swung and went for his second revolver, but he was a natural left-hander and fumbled the draw. Practice of the border shift had enabled him to change hands quickly when such a situation as this arose, but that was when no danger threatened, and this was the first occasion he had been forced to use it in the heat of the moment. And it looked like it would be his last.

Burnett's gun blasted at the exact moment Angus managed to palm his own gun in his left hand. The deputy spun round, blood spurting from a head wound. Luckily it was only a crease as the outlaw's injured shoulder had soured his aim. Burnett was not so fortunate, however, as Angus managed to trigger off a shot before he fell to the ground. It was a lucky chest shot, and sealed the bandit's fate. He keeled over and lay still. Waxy Bennett would not be enjoying the dubious pleasures of Brown's Park after all.

Amidst the hectic affray, Fresno had decided that he was no match for the tough BAD agent and his two-gun sidekick, and he quit the scene pronto. Unseen by the other participants, he quickly disappeared into the undergrowth. Only when the fight was over did Drew realize his absence. 'Did you see which way he went?' he rapped out, snatching up Burnett's abandoned hand gun and panning across the killing ground. But Angus was in no state to have noticed.

Any thought of going after the fleeing villain was delayed as he attended to his pard's wound, using the deputy's own bandana as a bandage to staunch the bleeding. It was some time before Angus regained consciousness. 'You sure were lucky there,' Drew asserted, dribbling water into his mouth. A stern frown, however, replaced the sympathetic manner when he knew his associate was out of danger. 'But all that fooling around with the gun sure had my heart beating faster than a Comanche war drum. What in tarnation were you playing at? That weren't no time for performing crazy tricks.'

'S-sorry about th-that, Drew,' the young man apologised with a nervous stammer. 'I never have been able to use my right hand properly. I keep practising, but don't seem to make much progress.'

'At least you came good in the end,' Drew said, tempering his admonishment with a wry smile. 'If'n you hadn't turned up at that moment, Burnett would have cut me down for sure. As it is he won't be causing no more bother to anybody. But there's still Fresno on the loose. You stay here and get down some of that grub they've cooked up while I go hunt him out.' And with that, Drew borrowed one of the outlaw mounts and headed off into the brush.

He was back an hour later empty-handed. 'Can't find hide nor hair of the turkey,' he said somewhat glumly. 'And the varmint even had the brass neck to steal the Barbary. He's skedaddled. No chance of catching him now. But at least I can take Burnett back to Laramie and claim the reward. I'll send half

41

to you, care of the sheriff's office in Bridger.'

Angus's face lit up. But the elation of receiving his first reward share was tempered by a more sombre mood. 'That's the first man I've killed, Drew. And even though it was him or me, it makes me feel sick in the stomach.'

'I know how you feel,' Drew commiserated, laying a comforting hand on the boy's shoulder. 'But the law has to take its course. And if'n rats like that are gonna shoot back, you ain't gotten no choice but to defend yourself and those you are commissioned to protect. Folks depend on guys like us to keep them safe. Just remember that the next time it happens.'

Such a commonsense explanation made Deputy McVay feel much better. After cramming down the food left by the outlaws, Drew mounted up on Fresno's abandoned cayuse with Bennett strapped over the saddle of his own mount.

Soon after, the two compadres said their farewells, Drew heading back to Laramie, while Angus continued west to take up his new appointment in Bridger.

CHAPTER FIVE

WELCOME TO BRIDGER

A week later found Angus crossing the Divide. Congratulating himself on having safely negotiated the broken terrain encompassing the Steamboat Bluffs, he dropped down to a barren plain of alkali flats. According to a sign he passed, his destination was only a further ten miles due west. Thankfully the trail cut across the eastern quarter of what looked like a waterless pale yellow desert. A silent prayer was despatched upwards expressing his heart-felt gratitude that he had made it. Not bad for a lone tenderfoot traveller.

Bridger was named after the famous mountain man. The young deputy felt himself honoured to have acquired a position in a town dedicated to such a renowned character from the old frontier days.

Maybe he would even meet him and split the breeze
with the old jasper. A contented smile graced his
youthful countenance as he pressed on, eager to
reach the town.

A cloud of white dust in the heart of the flats
caught his attention. And it was moving his way at a
fair lick. As it drew closer Angus saw that it was a herd
of around a hundred cattle being driven by a trio of
drovers. And they appeared to be in a hurry. But
what were cowboys doing driving cattle across this
inhospitable terrain in the first place? Certainly not
the way for responsible cow hands to be moving
cattle.

Angus steered his horse across to intercept the
drovers. At close quarters he had never seen a
sorrier-looking bunch of steers. Ribs poked out of
skin hanging loose on the poor critters. The cowpokes were none too pleased at having to curtail
their progress for some prying nosebag. 'Looks like
we got company, Rufe,' a bearded hardcase shouted
across to one of his buddies, on spotting the intruder
bearing down on them.

Rufe Kegan threw a resentful look towards the
approaching rider. 'That's the last thing we need,' he
grumbled. 'Some nosey drifter queering our pitch.'
Nonetheless he pulled up to meet the intruder. 'Half
Pint,' he called across to the smallest of the trio – the
nickname was obvious to anyone encountering the
stunted cowpoke – 'Keep these critters moving while
me and Bull sort out this snooper. We need to get
'em settled in the hidden valley by sundown.'

44

Kegan and his pard Bull Braddock waited with scowling faces as the newcomer approached. Angus peered at the dispirited bunch of beeves. 'Howdie, boys,' he said; then trying not to sound critical: 'Those steers look mighty short on meat. I hope you don't mind me saying, but pushing 'em like that ain't gonna bring you much dough at auction.'

'We do mind, fella,' Kegan snorted twisting his lip. 'Telling us how to run a bunch of steers ain't none of your concern.'

'Just trying to give some friendly advice, is all,' Angus replied shrugging his shoulders. 'If'n it ain't wanted, I'll just push on my way.' He swung his horse away from the surly duo, wondering what these jaspers were up to.

'Yeh, you just do that.' Braddock grunted. Once the interloper was out of earshot, he turned to his buddy. 'You don't suppose he suspected what we were doing, do you Rufe?'

'No chance,' Kegan scoffed. 'He's just some meddling kid who figured we were greenhorn cowpokes. And that's how I like it. Now let's catch up Half Pint. Sooner we're off these darned flats and into grass country the better.'

'He sure was right about them needing to be fattened up,' Braddock remarked, casting a jaundiced eye towards the disappearing plume of white dust. 'No way will those buyers we've arranged be willing to pay up with them like this.'

'We didn't have no choice,' Kegan answered irritably. 'You know darned well this was the only way off

45

the Lazy K range without us being spotted. So let's get moving. The isolated grass valley we found is only a half day's drive through that draw over yonder.'

Braddock's untimely complaint had soured Kegan's mood. 'Your turn to ride drag, Bull,' he smirked. 'Don't eat too much sand.'

The big man grumbled some. But you didn't refuse when Rufe Kegan gave orders. He was running this show. Braddock pulled his necker up over his mouth and nose to keep out the constant swirl, and vanished into the fermenting maelstrom. With Half Pint riding left point, Kegan took the right, pushing the herd until they were almost running so as to reach the hidden valley before any other snooping intruders could interfere.

He made sure to keep the lead steer up front. The key element in pushing small herds, indeed any size of herd, was to select a pacemaker that all the others would follow. It made the job of driving the cattle that much easier, an essential factor with only three of them to drive the stolen herd.

When Angus reached Bridger two hours later, his presence was soon spotted by an old-timer leaning against the side of the sheriff's office. One of Coonskin Radley's jobs was to report the arrival of any strangers arriving in the border town. His other was to act as night watchman at the jail when any prisoners were being held. Since retiring as a trapper, much of his free time had been spent propping up the bar at the Plainsman saloon across the street. He was grateful to Sheriff Vince Sublette for giving him the job.

The trademark top covering, the origin of his nickname, had never been known to leave his head. When asked about it, he claimed it kept the sun off his bald pate. Then he invariably launched into tales of the rip-roaring times spent at the Green River rendezvous where beaver pelts were traded. Those days were long gone, as was most of the trapped-out beaver. Most guys in his occupation had been forced to seek alternative employment. But Coonskin was a fluent raconteur, and the much embellished stories bought him plenty of free drinks in the Plainsman.

'Come on out here, sheriff,' he called in a scratchy voice coarsened by too much whiskey. 'We got company.' A lean-limbed man, tall and broad-shouldered, emerged from the office. Coonskin pointed to the eastern end of the main street. 'Stranger coming in. Looks like some saddle tramp to me.'

'Could be the new deputy I'm expecting,' Sublette announced in a less than enthusiastic tone of voice. 'He's due in any day.'

'You don't sound too pleased,' his assistant commented, picking up on the noncommittal reaction to the newcomer.

'The town council reckon I need a new deputy to protect the Overland stage line that's opened recently.' Vince Sublette cast a jaundiced eye towards the newcomer. 'He sure has the trail-busted look of what you said, Coonskin. And young, too. How am I expected to stop ruthless road agents when I have to

47

nursemaid some hick tenderfoot?'

There was no denying that Angus McVay was not looking his best. It had been a tough journey from Rock Springs – the rugged terrain and crossing the Divide had taken a lot out of both man and beast. And then there was that fracas with the Silver Dollar boys. But at least he had made it unscathed, save for a bandage round his head. The wound had healed, even though it had left him with a distinct groove in his scalp. He quickly removed the bandage and stuffed it in his jacket. The last thing he wanted was to have to explain how he had come by the injury.

And just in the nick of time, as well. Some way down the main street, he noticed a raw-boned jasper step down off the boardwalk and look his way, and on drawing closer the shiny tin star informed him that this had to be his new employer. Even though he was dog tired and in need of a hot bath, not to mention a good sleep, Angus shook off his lethargy and squared his shoulders. He needed to make a good first impression.

Dusting off the alkali as much as he could, Angus dismounted and walked his cayuse over to where the sheriff was waiting. 'The name's Angus McVay, sheriff,' he introduced himself. 'I'm the guy you're expecting.'

Sublette likewise shook off his previous cool manner, instead presenting the appearance of an enthusiastic officer of the law eager for his new deputy's support. 'Glad to have you join us, Angus,' he enthused, putting on a beaming smile of welcome. 'I've fixed you up with a room at Ma Docherty's rooming house on Carson Street. And there's a stall ready for your horse at the livery stable. Get yourself settled in and report to me first thing in the morning, and I'll acquaint you with your duties.'

'Ain't you gonna introduce me, sheriff?' old Coonskin butted in, scratching at his raggy beard. 'Seeing as how me and this young shaver will be working together.'

'My mistake,' Sublette apologized. 'Angus McVay, meet Coonskin Radley, the best turnkey in Caribou County. He's a mite long in the tooth, but nobody has ever escaped from the jail since Coonskin took over.'

'Pleased to meet you, Coonskin,' Angus said, accepting the hand of welcome. 'You look like a fella that's done some hunting in his time.'

'Don't get the old-timer on that,' Sublette interrupted, 'or we'll be here until the cows come home.'

Coonskin chuckled. But he was still proud to know that his presence at the jail was valued. Nonetheless he still wanted the newcomer to understand that Coonskin Radley had all his marbles at home. 'In my day I was the best hunter and trapper this side of the Grand Tetons. But don't you be thinking I'm past it, young fella,' he asserted poking a finger in Angus's chest. 'Ain't nobody gets the better of me around here.'

'You're durned right there, Coonskin,' Sublette agreed. 'You go see Ma Docherty, Angus. Ain't nobody in Bridger makes a finer apple pie. See you in the morning.' And with that, the sheriff retired to the office, leaving Coonskin to take his new deputy down to the livery stable and subsequently along to his accommodation.

And Ma Docherty's place proved to be an ideal lodging house. An initial reflection after the evening meal while lying on his bed told Angus that he had landed on his feet securing this job. And he fully intended to make his presence felt.

CHAPTER SIX

NO PLAIN SAILING

Over the following few days Angus acquainted himself with the town, introducing himself around the place while getting to grips with his responsibilities. It was on the fourth day that a somewhat puzzling incident occurred, one that did not sit quite right in the new deputy's limited experience of how the law should be administered.

A fight had taken place in the Plainsman saloon. It was the culmination of a festering dispute between two homesteaders. Like many such arguments, an over-indulgence of hard liquor had caused the simmering resentment finally to boil over when the two men clashed in the saloon. Loud words and death-dealing threats saw the owner of the Plainsman hustling over to the law office for help. Without knocking he burst through the door into the office, where Angus was studying the latest batch of Wanted dodgers.

The deputy was alone, his boss having been ensconced in the office of Judge Farthing for the last hour. Angus had just turned over a 'wanted' face he would have recognized had he not been suddenly interrupted. The dodgers were forgotten, stuffed in the desk drawer, when he observed the worried look on Crackerjack Clem Alty's face. 'You gotta come quick, sheriff,' the wafer-chewing barman babbled, wiping stray crumbs from his sweating red face. 'Grizzly Frank Dodge and Tom Behan are all set to blast each other apart over yonder.' He slung a thumb towards the saloon. 'They've gotten into a fracas about water rights that's been bubbling for months. And now it's about to explode in gunfire.'

A gleam of excitement registered in the young deputy's eyes. Here was a chance to prove his worth. Without uttering a word, Angus jumped to his feet and strapped on his twin-rigged gunbelt. 'You can count on me, Crackerjack,' he rasped. The raw tension such confrontations engendered had caused his voice to grind. He coughed to hide any apprehension. 'Now let's go enforce the law!' Affecting a confident manner, he hurried out the door, followed by the barman who was nervously nibbling at one of the crackers he always kept handy.

The source of the dispute was clearly audible. Raised voices and furious threats informed the lawman that swift action on his part was essential to quell any blood being spilled. Numerous bystanders had congregated outside the saloon, but at a safe distance so as not to be in the line of fire. Pewter-grey clouds scudding by overhead had set the tone of the scene by blotting out the harsh sunlight. Two dogs growled at each other, seemingly acting out the grim scenario inside the Plainsman.

Angus squared his shoulders. Sam Vender had always instilled in him the need for caution when approaching unknown dangers. Don't rush in before you know the score, he had insisted. Heeding the cogent advice, he paused outside the window of the saloon and peered inside the dimly lit room.

Only the two belligerent participants were visible. All other patrons had clearly sought sanctuary elsewhere. Angus palmed one of his matching Colt Peacemakers in the active left hand, and sidled through the door. Catlike so as not to unnerve the duellists, he sucked in a deep breath before barking out a firm order: 'Raise your hands,' was the cutting mandate, 'and don't either of you go for them hoglegs.'

Both men instantly ceased their aggressive jousting. Two startled faces, bearded, wrinkled and weather-beaten, faced the speaker. Clad in faded dungarees and slouch hats, they looked like a pair of stroppy brothers. But their scowling faces spoke of no filial accord. And no arms were raised. Hands still hovered menacingly over gun butts. Angus repeated his order. 'You heard me. Reach!' His gun lifted to emphasize his determination. 'You're both under arrest for disturbing the peace.'

The smaller and more mousey of the pair, Tom Behan, instantly complied. But his more bullish rival,

Grizzly Frank, scowled. He hawked out a scoffing guffaw. 'Disturbing the peace, eh? I'll sure disturb your peace, mossy horn.' His follow-up churlish remark was to his opponent: 'Don't be such a weak-kneed weasel,' he chidingly mocked his scrawny neighbour. 'Look at the guy. He's only some tender-foot kid trying to play the hero. We can easily take him. Then finish what we started.'

A common enemy seemed to have tempered his dispute with Behan, at least temporarily. The angry hulk lumbered across the room, his bear-like arms swinging ready to deliver a crunching blow. Had the haymaker landed, that would have been the end for Angus McVay, his job over before it had barely started.

A nifty side-step, however, and Angus brought his gun barrel down on the braggart's bullet head. It was not a hard blow, merely stunning the drunk. Dodge yelped, falling to his knees. 'I could have gunned you down, mister. Easy as pie,' Angus observed in a calmly delivered tone. His own gun remained fixed, unmoving, aimed at the caterwauling braggart. This jigger was so half cut it would have been pure murder to gun him down. 'But you ain't worth the mud on my boots. And stow that racket. You'll wake the dead.'

All of Angus's attention was focused on Grizzly Frank. Behan appeared to be thoroughly cowed by his forthright intervention. But the sodbuster's initial shock soon wore off. The mousey face now betrayed a cunning the young lawman had ignored in his elation at scoring a perfect result on the intimidator's bundled attack. Angus was buzzing, the adrenalin coursing through his lithe frame.

It was Crackerjack Alty who saved his bacon. The hawk-eyed bartender had spotted the devious leer on the sodbuster's grizzled face. 'Look out, sheriff,' he yelled from the doorway. 'Behan's got a knife.'

Angus had already sensed the clumsy movement away to his left, sunlight glinting off the deadly blade. He slewed to one side seconds after the knife sliced through a shirt sleeve. Caught off balance, the clumsy blockhead slewed into a table. The deputy's response was immediate. His left hand panned round punching out two shells. One lifted the weasel's hat, the other sliced a chunk from his left ear. 'Drop the shiv, mister,' Angus commanded, his voice strong and decisive. 'Another crazy stunt like that will buy you a hole in the cemetery.'

Even though drunk, Tom Behan was no fool and knew when to cash in his chips. The heavy knife hit the floor. Angus was annoyed, with himself more than the soused nester. 'OK, Behan,' he snapped out, eager to further his command of what could have been a risky showdown. 'Help your crazy pal over to the jail. Drunk and disorderly has now been promoted to violent affray. You boys are going down for quite a spell in the hoosegow when the judge tries your case.' With both guns pointing unerringly at the backs of the sombre troublemakers, Angus called for somebody to find a sawbones to attend their injuries.

A crowd of muttering citizens followed the stumbling duo as they staggered down the street. 'Well done, sheriff,' one bystander remarked. 'Those two deserve a spell in the cooler.' Angus smiled to himself. He had come out on top, and at the same time learnt a valuable lesson. The show ain't over until the final curtain falls.

When they reached the jailhouse, Sheriff Sublette arrived at the double. 'What's all the shooting about?' he enquired. 'I was in conference with the judge when we heard all the commotion.'

The man in question had followed him down the street. Judge Malachi Farthing was a rotund official with prominent grey side whiskers sprouting from a full head of well coiffured hair parted down the middle in the latest fashion. He had a large cigar clutched betwixt finger and thumb. Here was a man of affluence as well as influence in Bridger. After Angus had explained the circumstances leading to the arrest, the judge immediately took charge. 'Bring them over to the courthouse straightaway, sheriff,' he ordered briskly. 'Then we can settle this matter without further ado. You come as well, deputy, to give your evidence.'

The case was cut and dried. Dodge and Behan both pleaded guilty, hoping by doing so to sustain a reduced sentence. But Judge Farthing was nothing if not determined to stamp out rowdy behaviour in his town. 'We will not stand for this sort of disorderly conduct in Bridger,' he asserted firmly, banging his gavel down hard on the desk. 'You turkeys are hereby sentenced to serve five years hard labour in the county prison at Sweetwater. And I will be recommending that no parole be considered.'

The men's vociferous grievance regarding the harsh ruling was quashed by the judge, who was all set to increase the term of incarceration. The hard-eyed threat soon stifled any further remonstration from the aggrieved prisoners.

'You get about your business, deputy, now this matter has been settled,' the official said. 'Me and the sheriff will see these two reprobates are firmly installed in the jailhouse until such time as we can arrange transportation to the penitentiary at Sweetwater.'

Before Angus departed Sublette drew him aside for a quiet word. 'Until you settle into the job, Angus,' he whispered in a firm yet meaningful way, 'it would be best if'n the gunplay was left to me. Can't have my new deputy getting himself shot up, can I?' He finished the veiled reprimand with a curt laugh to show there were no hard feelings.

Angus merely nodded, leaving the courthouse nursing a somewhat deflated void in his stomach. There was also a feeling of sympathy for the prisoners. The men had been drunk and acting brash, but had in truth posed little harm. Admittedly, his life could have been in danger had not Crackerjack Alty intervened. But even then, he had already spotted the blundering attempt by Tom Behan to cut him up with a knife. And due to his soused condition the aim was way off beam anyway.

And then there was the judge's circumvention of a jury. It was almost like the town was being subject to officially sanctioned vigilante law. Angus was wandering down the main street mulling over the harsh sentence when a man approached him.

'Pleased to meet you, Deputy McVay,' the official said, breezily holding out his hand. 'Sorry I wasn't around when you arrived. Duty calls, you understand.' He did not elaborate. 'The name is Cyrus Gillan. I'm the Mayor of Bridger and leader of the town council.' A man of medium height in his fifties, smart as behoved his lofty position, Gillan's lean visage sported a neatly trimmed beard and moustache that was waxed at the ends.

Angus accepted the greeting cordially. But there was something about the man that was nagging at his memory. He felt deep down an acquaintanceship he just could not place. 'You seem familiar, Mister Mayor,' he said warily. 'Have we met some place before?'

The administrator frowned, mulling over the query. 'Not that I can recollect,' he replied. 'Maybe you have mistaken me for someone else.'

The explanation was acknowledged with an understanding shrug. 'Guess that must be it. Judge Farthing sure takes his job seriously. I wouldn't want to come up before him for littering the street.'

The mayor nodded his agreement. 'He does seem to have a liberal view of how the law should be enacted. Some malefactors get off with a light fine, while others have the book thrown at them. But together, he and Sheriff Sublette have done a good job of keeping the riff-raff out of Bridger. And for that we should be grateful.' He then changed the subject. 'Anything you need to make your job easier, just let me know.'

And with that, both men continued on their way. Angus needed a drink to settle his nerves following the troubling incident in the Plainsman, not to mention its bizarre aftermath.

With Dodge and Behan in the lock-up awaiting the prison wagon that would take them to Sweetwater, the incident subsequently took second place in favour of his getting to grips with the new job. Angus was settling in nicely and enjoying his new routine when some days later he happened to meet up with Mayor Gillan once again. On this occasion the older man was hurrying down the street and appeared a mite flustered.

'You seem in a hurry, Mayor Gillan. Is there something wrong?' As he asked the question, Angus was once again studying the man's bearded face carefully, his brow furrowed in thought. That face certainly was familiar, but he was hanged if'n he could place it. The mayor's worried look made him pretty sure it was no figment of his imagination.

'Have you seen the sheriff?' the mayor gasped out. 'He's not in his office and I need to speak with him urgently.'

'I ain't seen Vince for a couple of hours, your worship. But if'n it's a legal matter, maybe I can help,' he offered.

No further chance of mulling over the conundrum was possible as the official blurted out his disturbing news. 'I've just spotted three hardcases going into the livery stable. I heard them ask the ostler if'n the sheriff was around. They were all tooled up and looking for trouble. And my reckoning is that they're after a showdown with Sublette.' The mayor was agitated and clearly fearful for the lawman's safety. 'We have to warn him.'

With Vince Sublette unavailable, Angus figured he had been given another opportunity to raise his profile – and no further time was given to chewing over the possibility. His gaze followed the mayor's pointing finger. 'There they are now, and heading this way.' Sweat was bubbling on the official's brow. 'What we gonna do?'

Angus adjusted his twin-rigged gun-belt, making sure his left hand was well flexed in readiness for the coming showdown. Facing down three hard-nosed varmints ought to have made him hesitate, yet he felt strangely calm, detached, ready to do his duty. As the trio drew closer, a furrowed ridge of puzzlement creased his forehead. 'I've met these birds before,' he remarked. 'Out on the flats east of here. They were pushing a bunch of steers at too fast a pace.'

'That's Rufe Kegan,' the mayor nervously croaked. 'And those two jaspers with him are Bull Braddock and Half Pint Lacey. Easy to tell them apart.' The curt guffaw lacked any hint of amusement. 'And you can bet those steers had been stolen off some poor rancher. They must have been moving them to better pasture. A couple of months back the sheriff caught them red-handed rustling cattle. They were locked up, but somehow managed to escape. Looks like they're out for revenge with Vince in their sights.'

The rustlers had not noticed Angus in the shadow of an overhanging veranda. He was about to step out into the open and make his challenge when the lean-limbed figure of Vince Sublette appeared from an alleyway on the opposite side of the street. He was accompanied by his pal the judge. The notion flicked through Angus's mind that these two appeared to be mighty close.

No time was given to further consideration of the unsettling liaison as the sheriff made his play. 'You jaspers looking for me?'

The confrontation was no more than a casual drawl. But it was enough for the three owlhoots to spin round, hands grabbing for the guns on their hips. The sheriff's response was immediate. Both guns leapt into his hands, orange flame spitting out hot lead. Spurts of sand exploded at the feet of the startled thieves. Another brief flurry of slugs lifted the hat from Kegan's head and snapped a jiggle-bob off Bull Braddock's left boot.

In the time it takes to say Dance with the Devil, the overwhelmed brigands were doing just that in the street, capering around like marionettes. 'Draw those guns, boys, and by thunder I won't be so careful with my next salvo of shots.'

Kegan knew he was beaten and immediately raised

his hands. 'OK Sheriff, you're too darned good for us.' Following their leader's directive, the other two did likewise. Without even a single shot having been fired off by the browbeaten crooks, the gun battle, if'n it could be so called, was over. Angus could only stand and stare agog, astounded that it had been so simple. Vince Sublette sure knew his business, there could be no denying that fact. Even Judge Farthing had not bothered to conceal himself from any flying lead, such had been his faith in the sheriff's prowess.

The rotund court administrator now stepped forward to congratulate the man of action. 'Well done, Sheriff,' he waxed lyrical, drawing his own revolver to show he meant business. 'The county has been plagued by these varmints for too long already.' He then turned his attention to the browbeaten gun-slingers while Angus was removing their hardware. 'Figured you could raise your standing among others of your odious breed, eh boys? Well you've over-stepped the mark and no mistake by taking on Vince Sublette. March them over to the courthouse, Sheriff, and we'll make their arrest official. You fellas are going down for a long spell.'

Before the deputation could disperse, Angus tried to gain his boss's attention. 'Reckon there's something you need to know, sheriff,' he said.

Before he could continue, Sublette cut him short. 'Not now Angus. As you can see, I'm busy.'

'I only wanted to say that . . .'

But the lawman was impatient to get his prisoners over to the courthouse. 'Later, OK? These jaspers need to be brought to trial and sentenced. I'm sure you have plenty to do while the court is in session.' And with that he turned away and marched the prisoners down the street.

'No point in buttonholing the sheriff, young fella, when his mind is occupied.' The croaky advice came from Coonskin Radley. 'He's a mighty fine peace officer but not the most patient of guys.'

Angus was even more puzzled now than he had been before. He stared after the crowd that was accompanying the prisoners down to the court house. Everybody enjoyed a good court case, so they were all eager to witness the due process of law being enacted from the safety of the public gallery. The young deputy couldn't help surmising that the three rustlers had given up rather too easily. And facial expressions that should have been downcast and dejected were anything but. Indeed, he had spotted Rufe Kegan exchanging a sly smirk with Half Pint Lacey.

Something was most definitely not right here.

CHAPTER SEVEN

GOOD ADVICE

He had no further chance to figure out what was happening when Mayor Gillan interrupted his disturbed thought pattern. 'Reckon I know what's bothering you, Deputy,' he declared. 'You wanted to tell him about the cattle they were driving across Alkali Flats. It's odds on those steers weren't acquired legally. But they've most likely been sold on by now.'

The mayor's interpretation of his grimacing look was only partially right. Angus didn't expound on his suspicions regarding the captured rustlers, merely explaining what he had seen on the Flats. 'I don't think they'll have been sold yet. My hunch is they're being held someplace in secret until they find a buyer. The brand they were carrying was a letter K on its side. If'n I find them, we'll know who they belong to.'

The mayor's face lit up. 'That's the brand used by

Charlotte Kimmel who runs the Lazy K. Since her husband was killed last year trying to stop a gang of rustlers, Charlotte has kept the spread going on her own with the help of an old cowpoke called Rooster Brown. Their ranch is in the valley of Elkhead Creek south of here in the foothills.'

'Then that's where I'll start my search,' Angus announced. 'Much obliged for your help, Mister Mayor. Can you tell Vince where I've gone? I hope he don't figure I'm overstepping my responsibilities.'

'My betting is that he'll be mighty pleased that his new deputy is showing such initiative.' The two men shook hands. Angus held the other man's piercing gaze. Even though the mayor was friendly and supportive, that nagging doubt still persisted that they had met up before. And he could lay odds it wasn't on friendly terms. But this was not the time to be pressing the issue.

The mayor had taken the puzzled frown to indicate the young law officer wanted directions to the ranch. 'Take the main trail south towards a distinctive tower of rock bursting out of the plains called Shoshone Butte. You'll understand why when you see it. Take a left beyond the Butte. That will lead you into Elkhorn Creek. Charlotte's place is half way down where it opens out into grazing country.' A smile cracked the angular face of the older man. 'Try and get there around noon. That gal makes the finest steak and onion pie you ever did taste.'

'Maybe the good lady will have some idea of where those beeves were taken,' Angus said. 'Driving them too hard across Alkali Flats had made the weight drop off'n those beeves. Good grass in a secluded place would be the only way to get them back up to scratch, that's for sure. And that takes time.'

'Then you'd better get started right away,' the mayor declared. 'It's a good three-hour ride to the Lazy K. And I'll make sure that Vince knows where you've gone. Although I'd best not tell him you're hoping to stay for lunch.' The deputy's knitted eyebrows saw the official adding warily, 'Vince has a soft spot for Charlotte, and he don't take kindly to other guys paying her attention, no matter how innocent.'

'In that case, perhaps it would be advisable to head straight across the flats without stopping.' Angus was coming to the conclusion that there was far more to Sheriff Sublette than he had figured. Not all of it good. 'I'll pack in some beef jerky and eat on the move.'

'I reckon that might well be the best option,' Gillan nodded sagely.

Angus thanked the mayor for his advice and went off to check his horse had been fed and watered for a lengthy ride. Fifteen minutes later, with the trial of the three rustlers in full swing, he passed the packed courthouse, pointing his horse to the south. He had much to occupy his mind. Not least the rather unsettling view slowly coalescing as to the character of his new boss. A solid lawman to be sure, but there were underlying issues that bothered the young deputy, and at some point in the near future he would have to decide whether he really wanted to partner such a shadowy and enigmatic personality.

But for now, he needed to concentrate on finding that stolen herd.

It was two hours later that he came across the bold upthrust of Shoshone Butte. A smile creased the young man's face. Did all Indians have such protruding noses? Just beyond the distinctive landmark, a wagon could be seen pulling out of the side trail leading to Elkhorn Creek. And it was being driven by a woman. This must be the alleged lady friend of Sheriff Sublette, and owner of the Lazy K. He breathed a sigh of relief. At least now the decision as to whether or not he should stop at the Lazy K ranch had been removed.

The wagon pulled to a halt as he approached, the driver displaying a firm competence at handling a feisty team. A comely woman pushed back her wide-brimmed Stetson, revealing long flowing auburn hair tied back in a red bow. Drawing closer, Angus could readily understand why the sheriff would be jealous of any man muscling in on his supposed territory. Charlotte Kimmel was not in the first flush of youth, but the sheriff's interest in her was understandable, even to a young sprout like Angus McVay. Fine lines branching out across velvety arched features enhanced rather than detracted from her obvious beauty.

She waited for him to draw level before offering a cheery greeting. Even when the newcomer was still a hundred yards distant, the woman had spotted the glint of metal on his chest. 'You must be the new deputy assigned to our *famously illustrious* sheriff,' she declared in a silky voice that matched her sensual appearance. 'Welcome to Caribou County and the town of Bridger.' The greeting was genuine, although the emphasis placed on her portrayal of the lawman appeared to be somewhat mocking.

Angus did not dwell on the notion as he accepted the proffered hand. 'Pleased to meet you, Mrs Kimmel,' he replied with a corresponding smile. 'I was on my way to speak with you about those steers that have been rustled.'

Charlotte's eyes arched with surprise. 'Well, I'm glad that somebody has seen fit to go after the culprits. I reported them missing over a week ago. And how do you happen to know they were my steers?'

Angus quickly appraised the woman about his meeting with the rustlers and what poor condition the steers were in, and explained that when he had mentioned the incident to Mayor Gillan, it was he who had told him who owned the brand. The arrest of Kegan and his sidekicks in Bridger for confronting the sheriff confounded the woman even more. 'Why would such men come to the town to confront our renowned gun-fighting sheriff?' she queried with a shake of the head. 'It doesn't make any sense.'

'Perhaps they reckoned that three against one were good odds in their favour,' the deputy suggested. 'Or maybe it was to fill time while those cows were feeding on good grass. One thing is for sure, it was a bad decision on their part.'

'I'm heading into Bridger now to stock up on supplies,' Charlotte said. 'If'n I see Vince, I'll let him know where you're headed.'

BAD GUY – ROUGH JUSTICE

'That's the problem, ma'am,' Angus averred warily. 'I ain't sure. That was my main reason for coming to see you. I figured you might have a better idea than me where these rustlers might have stashed the herd. It'll need to be an isolated place with plenty of good grass, one where they ain't likely to be spotted while putting on weight.'

The woman's eyebrows met in the middle as she carefully considered the request. 'If'n they were headed across Alkali Flats when you ran into them, they'll have been heading for one of the numerous draws on the far side. There's plenty of good grazing land over that way that nobody owns. Although that can only be a matter of time. Cattle are becoming big business in Wyoming.' Then another thought occurred to her. 'You're gonna need some proper chow if'n you plan to cross that barren wasteland. Call at the ranch on your way past and tell Rooster Brown, my foreman, I said for him to see you right.'

'That's mighty decent of you, ma'am,' Angus said. 'I never figured it would be such a long trip away from town.'

'Two, maybe three days at least,' the rancher surmised. 'The Flats ain't to be taken lightly. And I'd be obliged if'n you could tell Chester, my son, that I want a full supply of wood chopping before I return. He's been spending too much time recently whittling with that knife old Rooster gave him.'

Angus couldn't resist a hearty laugh. In the brief period of their acquaintance, this tough yet warm-hearted woman had certainly exerted a mesmeric charm on him. Not in a physical sense – she was old enough to be his mother. He only wished that his mother could have survived that fatal illness long enough to display the same element of human kindness.

Before they parted company, he added a rather hesitant postscript. 'If'n you don't mind, ma'am, I'd take it kindly for you not to mention our meeting to the sheriff.'

Charlotte frowned. 'Why not?' she asked stiffly, exhibiting a baffled curl of the lip.

The reply was restrained, diffident. 'I'm sorry, but I was warned that he might get a bit . . . well, jealous of other men talking to you. Even a young shaver like me.' The nervous laugh that followed was an attempt to play down the embarrassing request.

A deep flush suffused the woman's cheeks, and her lips compressed into a thin line of anger. The reaction when it came was harsh and to the point. 'If'n Vince Sublette figures he's gotten a hold on me, he has another think coming. I'll speak with who I darned well please. And whenever I please. Who does that critter figure he is? Nobody tells Charlotte Kimmel what to do, least of all a gun-slinging sheriff. Of all the nerve.'

The vitriolic diatribe fizzled out as soon as it had been delivered when she heeded the young deputy's ashen discomfort.

'Don't be thinking this is aimed at you, Angus. You come round to the ranch whenever you want. And I'll be pleased to see you . . . whatever Vince high-

and-mighty Sublette may think.' These last words were almost spat out.

Peace and harmony having been restored, the pair of newfound allies bade farewell to each other. 'And you be sure to tell Rooster to give you some of those fresh biscuits I made this morning,' Charlotte said breezily, anxious to depart on a cordial note. 'He'll huff some 'cos they're his favourite. But he's all heart, really. A godsend since my husband Rance died.'

The Lazy K ranch was a further hour's ride south from Shoshone Butte. The spread was isolated amidst a cluster of cottonwoods acting as windbreaks. Well-fed cattle were grazing leisurely on the surrounding land. These were prime beef steers that would fetch a good price at market. Rufe Kegan and his gang had made a big error hurrying such fine beasts across the arid wasteland of the Flats. When he found them, Angus would enjoy nothing more than passing on the good news to the prisoners before they were shipped off to the pen at Sweetwater.

The ranch house itself was constructed of rough-hewn logs covered with a sod roof. A thick stone chimney at one end offered plenty of heat during the harsh winters that plagued Wyoming. Over in the corral, a grizzled man, an army veteran judging by his dark blue military hat, was busy with a branding iron. When he spotted the newcomer, Rooster Brown laid down the tools of his trade and came across. 'Something I can do for you, mister?' he said somewhat suspiciously before spotting the tin star. 'Ah, you must be the new guy,' he said, a smile spreading over the wizened features. 'We don't get many visitors out this way. Set down and I'll put the coffee on.'

Angus was impressed by the friendliness paid. 'Much obliged,' was his equally affable reply as the old guy went off to prepare the coffee. Ten minutes later Angus was lazing in a rocking chair on the porch when Rooster returned, carrying a tray of cookies. The deputy smacked his lips. 'Boy, they look good,' he exclaimed, selecting a tasty treat. 'You sure appear to have landed on your feet here, Rooster.'

'How'd you know my handle?' the puzzled foreman asked, creasing up an already wrinkled visage even more. 'We ain't met someplace before, have we?'

Angus shook his head, then went on to explain how he had met up with Rooster's boss on the trail, and that she had invited him to stop awhile. His follow-up remark was made somewhat cagily. 'She also said you'd oblige a friendly dude passing through with chow for his forthcoming journey. I'm heading out across Alkali Flats to look for those rustled steers.'

A sagacious nod from Rooster. 'I'm glad to see somebody has taken an interest,' the foreman opined. 'You'll need a full gunny sack to cross that blamed wilderness. Don't worry none, I'll see you right.' It was during this exchange of pleasantries that Angus received another disturbing piece of information when the foreman added an observation that saw his guest visibly stiffening in his seat. 'Although it's to be hoped you come back this way in one piece.'

'What d'you mean by that?' An unsettled look was aimed at his craggy host. 'Why in thunder shouldn't I come back?'

'Don't get me wrong,' Rooster replied, raising a hand. 'Vince Sublette is one tough law officer. But his deputies do seem to be accident prone. You're the third we've had in a year. Of the other two, one slipped down a gully and broke his neck. And the other just plain disappeared. All that was ever found was his hat on the rim of Arapaho Mesa.'

Any further conversation on the matter was interrupted by the arrival of Chester Kimmel. The boy was carrying a knife and a piece of half-carved wood. The unsettling revelation divulged by Rooster was shelved as he greeted the boy with a hearty, 'Howdie there, partner!' He went on to inform Chester of his mother's order. 'And she sure wasn't smiling when she said it,' he added winking at the chuckling foreman.

'Best get to it, boy,' Rooster advised, adopting a serious manner. 'You know what your ma's like if'n a job ain't done to her satisfaction.' Just like all boys, Chester grumbled and groused before ambling off to address the chore.

Soon after, with a gunny sack packed with goodies hanging from his saddle horn, Angus bade farewell to his generous host and headed off into the unknown. The last time he had stumbled upon the notoriously barren stretch was while skirting its eastern rim, where he had encountered Rufe Kegan and his pards. They had clearly crossed the arid expanse from here, pushing the herd fast to reach the far side and the next waterhole, and in so doing the beasts had lost much of their weight.

An hour later, Angus crested a rise, leaving the Elkhorn valley behind. Ahead of him lay the bleak prospect of alkali-covered flat-lands stretching away into the hazy distance. Angus uncorked a water bottle and took a couple of swigs. He was grateful to Rooster Brown for lending him a second canteen. He was going to need that extra life-giving elixir to traverse this desolate spread safely. Sucking in a breath of overheated air, he dropped down the back slope, immediately leaving behind the fertility of the Elkhorn country.

The dust-choked expanse, flat and lifeless, was sprinkled here and there with desiccated clumps of sagebrush. Such was the vastness of this sterile terrain that the far side was merely a hazy smudge on the horizon. Angus nudged the horse on to the hard-packed desert, walking the animal to conserve energy and moisture. At various intervals during the heat of the day, the dust-caked traveller dismounted to lead his mount.

He spent the night wrapped in his blanket to stave off the cold, as heat rapidly dissipated during the hours of darkness. Sleep had not come easily to the young tracker. His thoughts kept harking back to the grim warning from Rooster Brown concerning the previous occupants of the job. There was certainly some kind of shady business occurring in Bridger, and this thought unsettled him.

The false dawn gradually filled the eastern sky with a cool ochre backdrop, which soon mushroomed into a scintillating array of spectacular coloration. Purple, blue, orange-yellow and red streaks heralded the arrival of the golden orb, hauling itself over the scalloped moulding of the distant Steamboat Range. Angus was already on the trail before the full measure of the sun made its presence felt. The coolness of dawn was soon dispersed as yet another day of body-sapping heat took control.

Mid-afternoon saw the rider's alkali-crusted eyes focusing on a change of colour as the dull ochre of the desert finally surrendered to the faded green of a cluster of Joshua trees. Relief at having safely traversed the bleak expanse surged through his lithe frame. Maybe soon he would be able to find those hidden steers. Within the hour, he had left the desert behind and was entering a labyrinth of tree-cloaked hills intersected by small valleys, anyone of which would have been ideal for grazing cattle.

All were empty of the animals he sought. The searcher was beginning to think he had been mistaken in his assumption until he slid over the next ridge – and there below were upwards of a hundred beef cattle, grazing contentedly on the lush grass. Angus's heart lurched. He'd found them. Hustling down the slope, he soon made out the distinctive K lying on its side. So confident were the rustlers that nobody would chance upon their booty that they hadn't bothered to change the brand. This was further proof he needed to put those varmints away for a long spell.

Dusk was settling over the hidden valley. Angus was preparing to leave after checking that the herd were benefiting from their new quarters when the sound of a breaking twig caught his attention. Somebody, or some animal perhaps, had come up behind him. Narrowed eyes pierced the gloom of the tree cover, trying to tease out what had made the noise. The familiar profile of a rider resolved itself, pausing on the edge of his vision. 'Who's there?' he called out, somewhat alarmed by the presence of another human being in this far-flung spot.

The figure moved closer, allowing Angus to relax when he recognized the rider. 'Jeepers, you took me by surprise, creeping up like that. I figured you might be. . . .' The comment was chopped short by the thundering blast from both barrels of a shotgun. A ragged hole appeared in the middle of the deputy's chest. 'Aaaargh!!' He threw up his arms and tumbled from the saddle.

The killer nudged his horse forwards and dismounted. Casually he prodded the body with the shotgun. There was no movement. A smile of satisfaction never reached the cold-eyed gaze. Down in the valley cattle were balling in anxiety. They were starting to mill about in confusion, spooked by this sudden disturbance to their tranquil existence. Slain by a hand he had recognized, Angus McVay could not hear them. And the ragged hole in his chest was a sure sign that he never would.

CHAPTER EIGHT

BREAKOUT

When Drew Henry had parted company with Deputy McVay, the BAD agent had headed back to Laramie. His feelings were distinctly mixed. On the one hand the heinous rampaging of Waxy Burnett had been terminated. The dead outlaw was now wrapped in a slicker and strapped across the saddle of his horse. But his partner, Skinny Jim Fresno, had disappeared, and frustration ate at Drew's craw. He always balked at leaving a job unfinished.

No amount of questioning other law officers on the return journey had revealed any hint that the villain was still in this part of the country. Maybe he had seen the writing on the wall and had lit out for distant parts – but the thought that he had allowed the rat to escape made the BAD agent seethe with indignation. That said, he was sure that someday in the not too distant future, Jim Fresno would inevitably end his lawless mayhem swinging from a gibbet.

Director Wainwright was sympathetic to his agent's regret that the skunk had got away. 'It happens to us all, Drew. I remember losing Mad Murgo Fletcher when he fled to Robber's Roost back in seventy-two. Felt real bad about that.' The commiseration was meant to alleviate the younger man's dejection, but a hint of a smile was all the appreciation offered. 'We'll post dodgers across the territory and beyond,' the director promised. 'With an enhanced reward on offer, there'll be plenty of bounty hunters ready to sniff him out.' That was no consolation to Drew who felt that he had failed.

Being too embarrassed that a young deputy had saved his bacon, Drew did not explain the full reality of the situation, figuring to brush it under the carpet. Wainwright did not press the matter. 'I'll see the reward is mailed to the bank in Rock Springs when it comes through,' he confirmed. Once the official paperwork had been completed, Drew headed back to the ranch. This time he was all set to hang up his guns and settle down for good.

Famous last words, as they say, will always come back to haunt you – and only two weeks after his return the proverbial ghost returned. It happened while weeding his vegetable plot outside the ranch house. Marshal Sam Vender arrived with another letter. And yet again, the lawman's downcast expression heralded bad tidings. 'What is it this time, Sam?' he snapped impatiently. 'If'n it's another letter from the bureau it can go in the waste bin. I'm finished with gun-fighting. I specifically told the director after I dropped off Burnett's mangy carcase. . . .' Losing Fresno had made him feel like a failure.

He got no further as the agitated lawman interrupted. 'It ain't that, Drew. I received this wire and figured you needed to see it lickety-split.' He handed over the cable. 'And it don't make for easy reading.'

Drew's eyes popped as he read the brief yet edifying missive: *The Vender brothers have escaped from a work detail after killing a guard. Reliable sources indicate they are headed your way.* It was signed by Austin Pickett, governor, Sweetwater Prison. Just when he thought his life was settling down, this happens. He knew exactly what those two varmints had in mind. A spell in the pen had likely fostered their hatred of the principal agent responsible for their incarceration. And with a guard dead, they had nothing to lose.

'That means they could be here any day,' Drew spat out, tossing his weeding hoe on the ground in anger. 'And the varmints will have me in their sights. They sure ain't coming here to organize a Sunday school picnic, except to make hot lead sandwiches for me to chew on.' The attempt at levity failed to raise any trace of an accompanying smile.

'Don't be forgetting my part in sending them down,' Sam pressed home. 'None of those fellas ever had any time for me 'cos I refused to join the gang. Now that I'm town marshal, it's my job to face them.'

'No chance,' Drew stressed firmly. 'You ain't no gunslinger, Sam. This is my problem and I'll sort it.

79

You stay out of the way.'

'I'm the official law around here, Drew,' Sam insisted. 'Folks will expect me to prevent any revenge on the town they might be harbouring in those warped minds.'

Drew was equally adamant that it should be he alone who handled the problem. No matter how much this most peaceful of the Vender boys argued his case, Drew stressed with coherent reasoning that Sam should seriously consider his new wife and child. 'Since Ruth passed away, I ain't got no responsibilities any more,' Drew emphasized, and saw that his argument had struck a chord. 'Throwing your life away serves no useful purpose. And those guys wouldn't hesitate to gun down their own kin. Especially when he's taken to wearing the badge. The best thing you can do is stay home and look after your family.'

Before Sam had any chance to reply, Drew was packing away his gardening tools and heading into the house. A chest in the back room was his destination, where the more lethal tools of another trade had been secreted away.

With the forthcoming showdown imminent, the two men rode back to Rock Springs. No words were spoken, each musing on the grim realization that the peace and tranquillity of the Big Sandy Valley was soon to be blown apart once again. The acrobatic antics of a family of prairie dogs that would normally have lifted a dejected mood passed unnoticed. Only as they were approaching Rock Springs did Drew voice the strategy he had formulated during the sombre ride.

He pulled to a halt on the edge of town beside an abandoned shed. 'I'll wait here behind this wall until they arrive. If'n what the governor said holds water, it won't be long now.' When Sam wanted to stick around, Drew shook his head. 'Best if'n you head on into town and make sure nobody rides out this way. Make up something about the creek bridge being unsafe. We don't want a panic erupting when the storm breaks. Then get on home where you're needed most.'

Drew dismounted and led his horse into the corral. He removed his rifle from its boot and checked it was fully loaded. It was one of the latest 1873 centrefire Winchesters issued to BAD agents, and a superb long gun. Drew settled down to wait as his pal reluctantly departed. His gaze was fixed on the trail heading north-east towards Sweetwater, from where the Venders had escaped. The infamous jail was no more than a three-day ride away. These critters would be stoking up their urgent need to wreak vengeance on the rat who had shut them away in that stinking hole.

On thinking over the showdown he was intent on facing alone, Drew's grip tightened on the rifle. He must not take these murdering critters lightly. They were ruthless and crafty in equal measure, as was proven by their brutal escape from a chain gang. In a short while it could be him lying in a pool of congealed blood, allowing the surviving gang members to do their worst: at the trial, Abel Vender had issued a virulent curse on the town, promising to return and burn the place to the ground. An impotent threat at the time, it now boded ill should Drew's one-man stand be blown apart in a hail of bullets. The blood ran cold in his veins at the thought, particularly as the two surviving Venders might well have taken other convicts along with them after the escape.

All the watcher could do now was hold his nerve and face the challenge, like the BAD agent he was. *We Never Give Up* was the bureau's slogan, and Drew Henry had every intention of living up to it, come hell or high water.

He was girding himself to face the forthcoming affray when a single rider appeared round a bend a mile off. Drew stiffened, his resolute gaze focusing on the approaching rider. As the hazy outline coalesced into the recognizable figure of Abel Vender, Drew sucked in a deep breath and rose to his feet. The rifle was clutched across his chest as he stepped out into the open. Drew had no intention of skulking in the shadows. He would face this most bloodthirsty of the Venders face to face.

But where was his brother? Hog was nowhere to be seen. Could this be a trap to catch him unawares? Drew's eyes quickly panned the terrain, noting there was plenty of opportunity for an ambush to be launched against him. He backed off, once again concealing himself behind the wall. The notion suddenly struck home that maybe he had taken on too much, assumed too much. The clock was ticking. And Abel Vender was drawing closer.

A strengthened resolve saw the challenger resuming his position in the middle of the trail. That was when he was spotted by the incoming rider. A leery grin spread across the dirt-smeared countenance as Abel hauled rein some fifty yards distant. 'So they've sent the big man himself out to welcome me back into the fold,' the killer scoffed, displaying not the slightest hint of being intimidated. 'It saves me having to sniff out your mangy hide.'

Drew had heard it all before. Bully boys trying to scare him. It hadn't worked then, and it sure wouldn't work now. But he was concerned about the whereabouts of Hog Vender. 'That dog-eating glutton of a brother gone walkabout, has he?' Drew snapped back. 'Or more likely the cowardly skunk is just too plain scared to face a real gunfighter?'

Abel's smirk slipped. He shook his head in dejection. 'Poor jasper caught a bullet when we broke away from that chain gang. He'll be serving his full sentence. So I guess it's just you and me, BAD boy.' He slowly stepped down from his horse, and walked towards his hated adversary. 'I may have been locked up in the pen for three blasted years, but don't be thinking that has interfered with my gun hand. No sirrreee, I can take you easy as pie. So how we gonna play this? You holding a rifle on me don't seem fair.'

A thread of concern showed itself on Drew's furrowed brow. This turkey appeared mighty confident, too full of himself, if'n the truth be told. He had always figured that Cain Vender was the best draw expert with a six gun. Hog was the sneaky one, the back stabber. Yet here was Abel Vender, the glutton of the family, displaying not a care in the world. Drew's frown increased. An attribute not lost on his opponent. 'You look a mite worried, BAD boy,' Abel scoffed, flexing his fingers in readiness for the approaching showdown. 'Worrying that good old Abel here is no pushover in the gunfighting stakes? And so you should be.'

Drew moved away from the cover of the wall, leaving his rifle behind. There was something not right here. But then no further thought was given to Abel Vender's arrogant conduct. 'That's far enough, mister,' the convict rapped out, hunkering down ready to make his play. Slowly, so as not to precipitate any advance impulsive action, he pulled a silver dollar from his vest pocket. 'I'm gonna flick this into the air,' he called out. 'Soon as it hits the dirt, we go to shooting. Agreed?'

A nod from the baffled agent saw the coin spinning skywards. Each man hawkishly followed its parabolic trajectory with mesmerised attention that neither participant could avoid. Up, up, up it rose before arcing over to its zenith, then down and down, spinning and glinting in the sunlight like a twinkling star. Time appeared to stand still as the moment of reckoning rushed towards its destiny.

Seconds before the shiny coin hit the ground, the deep crack of a rifle sliced through the tense atmosphere. A scream of pain followed – and Hog Vender staggered out from behind a stack of boulders where he had been waiting to ambush the unsuspecting victim of the devious charade. He was still holding the rifle that would have killed him, and which he now tried to raise intending to finish the job so abruptly cut short. Another blast from the hidden rifleman and Hog went down, and stayed there.

His conniving plan unexpectedly thwarted, Abel emitted a startled cry of rage. But he quickly recovered. Even though his devious plot had been sussed and some sharp-eyed marksman had got Hog, he was not about to surrender now. That was a certain trip down Hellfire Alley with the hangman. 'Hog may be down, but I sure ain't,' he snarled, going for his own gun.

Although equally startled by this sudden change of fortune, Drew was ready for him. His own gun was palmed, bucking twice in rapid fire succession, the double tap dropping the charlatan where he stood. Slowly and with deliberate hesitancy he approached the still form, to check that the Grim Reaper had indeed made his mark.

A movement to his left saw the nervy agent spinning on his heel and dropping to one knee, his six-shooter pointing at the stomach of − Sam Vender, who was now emerging from where he had been secretly hiding in a nearby hut. He was holding a rifle across his chest, smoke twirling from the barrel. It was an old Springfield breech loader, well past its best, but it had always served him well, and had not failed him now.

Drew's whole body seemed to slump at the realization he had escaped certain death only through the calculated action of his associate. He was breathing hard, sucking air into tight lungs as he holstered his revolver. He bent over to regain his composure before gratefully thanking his saviour. 'Boy! That sure was a near miss,' he blurted out. 'If'n you hadn't spotted that sneaky toad hiding out there, I'd have been done for.' He paused once again to draw breath. 'For once I'm glad that somebody smarter than me disobeyed orders. I owe you my life, buddy.'

Characteristically Sam passed off the compliment as of no concern. 'I figured something was wrong when Abel turned up alone. No way would he face anybody like you on his ownsome. The guy is murderous, but a coward at heart.' Drew staggered across and hugged his pal with gratitude. These near-death encounters were becoming too much of a habit. 'I circled around behind the back lots, until I spotted where Hog was concealed,' Sam explained, having prised himself out of the bear hug. 'Then I waited for the right moment to let fly and spoil his dirty deed.'

'I reckon this calls for a few drinks at the saloon,' Drew declared. 'I sure need it to bring my nerves back to normal. That was a close shave I don't want repeated.' He then handed over his Winchester to the lawman. 'Reckon you need a decent rifle to do the job properly.' When Sam protested, Drew was resolute. 'I can get another from the agency,' he insisted. 'A good lawman needs the right tools to back him up. That old Springfield saved my bacon today, but I reckon it's due for retirement – like me.'

As the two buddies walked slowly back into Rock

Springs, citizens were emerging from their homes. A babble of conversation as to the cause of the shoot-out was aimed at the two protagonists. 'All in good time, folks,' Sam said, addressing the crowd. He had quickly passed the word for everybody to stay indoors until instructed otherwise. 'Give Mister Henry here some room to breathe. He just faced down and beat the two Vender boys who escaped from the penitentiary at Sweetwater a few days ago.'

Drew immediately rallied himself to remedy their marshal's blatant bending of the truth. 'If'n Sam here hadn't played his part in this showdown, I would have been a dead duck. You have a fine law officer here, folks.' He slapped Sam on the back. 'Make sure you back him up to the hilt.' He and Sam then pushed through the muttering crowd, eager to avail themselves of the saloon's liquor supply.

CHAPTER NINE

BAD NEWS FROM BRIDGER

The day after the heavy drinking spree, Drew didn't face the coming day until the afternoon. His head was throbbing. At least he had ended up in bed at the National Hotel. How he had got there, however, was something of a mystery. Dousing his head in cold water helped some way to alleviating the after effects – and the next thing that never failed to bring him round was a hearty breakfast.

Sam joined him at the Prairie Diner, feeling no less hung over, but cups of strong, hot coffee and a big fry-up soon made them feel like their old selves. 'I'll have the bodies packed up and sent back for burial in the jail cemetery,' Sam declared, puffing on a large cigar. 'Those two are not fit to end their days beside Ruth and our parents. What plans do you have now?' he enquired of his friend.

Drew thought about it for a spell. 'I'll need to write a report of the incident for the Bureau in Laramie, seeing as I was involved,' he replied pensively with a sigh. 'I know the director will try persuading me to accept another assignment. But this time I intend handing in my badge for good and walking away. No more putting my life on the line. I'm getting too old for that sort of thing. I've had more than my fair share, not to mention the scars that go with it.'

Bidding farewell to Sam, Drew headed back to the ranch, where he stayed the night before setting off early the next morning for his trip to Laramie.

When BAD director Theo Wainwright responded to the knock on his door, he was not surprised when the agent handed in his badge of office. Disappointment, reluctance, even a hint of exasperation creased his ageing face, as he tried unsuccessfully to hide his regret. Good agents of Drew Henry's calibre were hard to find, and his skill and experience were not easily passed on in training courses. His were inherent talents that few men acquired. 'I'll be sorry to lose you, Drew,' he murmured. 'Guys of your calibre don't come along very often.'

But Wainwright was nothing if not philosophical. Henry was getting on in years. And it was only fair that he be allowed to enjoy his life unsullied by the ever present danger of a bullet in the back. This was the end of the road, and they both knew it. Accordingly they shook hands, and Drew signed all the papers necessary for his termination of employment. They were saying their goodbyes when there was a knock on the door. A clerk entered the office and thrust a cable into Wainwright's hand. 'This just came in, sir,' the man said. 'I figured you'd want to know about it straightaway.'

Thick bushy eyebrows met as Wainwright perused the message with a degree of solemn gravity that immediately caught Drew's attention. 'Something bad happened, boss?' he asked. The director handed over the message.

After reading the brief yet devastating report, the blood drained from Drew's face. He read it a second time to be certain he was not hallucinating – *Deputy Peace Officer based in Bridger, Caribou County, shot dead in mysterious circumstances.* The grim truth remained the same, there in black and white: the dead peace officer had to be Angus McVay.

'Peace! That's a laugh!' Drew snorted, emitting a choked cackle of derision. Angus had only been in the job a short while, and now he was dead, gunned down by some murdering scumbag. Drew's blood ran cold in his veins. And what did it mean by *mysterious circumstances*?

The transparent angst displayed by his colleague elicited a terse reply from Wainwright. 'You know the victim?'

Drew swallowed down the bile swilling round in his gullet. His response was hesitant, guilt clouding the rugged features. 'I didn't exactly tell you the truth about the Silver Dollar episode, boss.' He gulped nervously, standing there twirling his hat like a kid caught with his fingers in the cookie jar.

Wainwright's face assumed a dusky cast. 'Best spit it out, Drew,' he said quietly.

'Fact is . . . it was McVay who shot Waxy Burnett when he and his pal almost nearly did for me.' He went on to outline the full facts of the bizarre incident. 'We parted company after that, and he carried on to take up his new job in Bridger.' A depressed mood settled over the big man's face. 'I didn't tell you at the time 'cos I was too ashamed when the slippery weasels caught me flat-footed. And when the reward comes through I was intending to send it all to him.' His head hung low. 'Well, that ain't possible now. So I shall donate it to the new hospital that's being planned for Rock Springs.'

The news of Angus's death was a brutal shock to the system. Yet another of his associates gunned down. Wainwright had listened quietly to the disclosure, not interrupting, and his reaction when it came was measured but fair; he observed: 'Never be ashamed about trying to maintain law and order. We all make mistakes. The main thing is to learn from them. I reckon you've done that. And forsaking any benefit does you credit.'

Before Drew could respond further to the untimely death of young McVay, the Director made an announcement that was to toss all his plans for retirement out of the window. 'McVay is the third

91

deputy to die in Caribou County in the last year.'
Once again the boss's temple knitted in serious
thought. 'Something ain't right over there, Drew.
One is to be expected occasionally, and two could be
put down as a coincidence. But *three* needs serious
investigation.' He looked at his associate silently,
willing him to take up the gauntlet.

'I'd count it as a great favour, sir, if'n you would
put my retirement on hold,' Drew solemnly asserted.
'Let me become the fourth deputy, and I'll suss out
what's going on.'

Wainwright's face lit up. 'That's what I was hoping
you'd say. Whoever is at the bottom of this is clearly
a shrewd jasper, and ruthless with it. You'll need all
your skill to bring this crook to justice.'

Drew left the BAD office with a job to fulfil. And
once again it had taken on a personal dimension.

He made good progress on a journey that was now
familiar territory. And so it was that five days after
leaving Laramie, Drew Henry found himself entering
the town of Bridger. On the surface an average sort of
berg, no better and no worse than a thousand others
scattered across the expanding western frontier. So
why had three deputies come to an untimely end in
such a short space of time? The notion nagged at his
brain as he walked his horse down the main drag.

Early on the agent had decided it would help his
cause to remain anonymous. The name of Drew
Henry was too well known in law enforcement agen-
cies throughout the territory and beyond – though

luck was on his side in that he had not ventured this far west before. Consequently Red Whyner received only curious glances as he rode down the main street, seeking out the sheriff's office. His objective initially was to play the greenhorn rookie when it came to law enforcement. That way he could make the culprits feel safe from any interference by the new man.

He tied up his horse and knocked on the office door. It was opened by an old-timer who introduced himself as Coonskin Radley. Drew made himself known.

'I'm the jailor, and the sheriff's eyes and ears,' the ageing turnkey declared proudly. 'Nothing escapes my notice in Bridger. Glad to have you join the team, Red.' A well lived-in face boasting more creases than a bloodhound gave him a puzzled look. 'Though it's a strange kinda handle for a jasper with black hair.'

Drew was ready for that one. 'My folks had a sense of humour and named me after my Uncle Silas, who brewed the finest beetroot whiskey you ever tasted.' Drew tried to keep a straight face as he got into his stride. 'Silas Whyner's Premium Red Label was famous throughout Kentucky. Can't have a better heritage than that, can I?'

'Well, I'll be doggoned!' the old timer exclaimed, scratching his bald pate. 'You're sure right there, boy. Any guy would be proud to have that kind of back-ground.'

The newcomer was about to reply when a raucous shout came from the rear of the cell block located down a short corridor to the rear. 'When we gonna get some grub, Coonskin?' a surly voiced growled out.

'And this time I want my steak medium rare, and heavy on the onions,' another chortling prisoner hawked out. Hilarious guffaws all round greeted this piece of biting wit.

'You'll get what you're given,' the turnkey snapped back, stamping his feet. 'Any more cracks and it'll be pigswill on your plates. So cut the jibes.' Silence followed. The old boy sniffed imperiously. Then in a loudly austere voice laced with satisfaction he counselled his new associate: 'You gotta be tough on these jaspers. Give 'em an inch and they'll eat your hand off.' What he failed to hear were the mocking sniggers emanating from the cell block.

At that moment, the sheriff himself appeared through the back door. 'Better take heed of the turnkey's warning, knuckleheads, or what he's suggesting will become reality.' Sublette's harsh threat soon chopped off the brazen hilarity from his prisoners. Only murmurings of discontent could be heard drifting out from the cell block. The sheriff closed the door to shut off any further interference.

He held out a welcoming hand. 'Vince Sublette, sheriff of Bridger, for my sins,' he declared breezily with a broad smile. 'Glad to have you with us, Red.' A cocked eyebrow lifted to the dark thatch atop the new man's head.

'I'll fill you in with the story later, boss,' Coonskin said. 'Best get down to the diner else these buzzards

BAD GUY – ROUGH JUSTICE

will start grumbling again. Although I don't see why they should be allowed to eat so well.'

'I've told you before, Coonskin,' Sublette methodically explained as if to a child. 'The judge has ruled that prisoners should be fed properly while awaiting trial or transportation to the county lock-up. "A contented prisoner causes less trouble guilty" is a good slogan to live by.'

'Still don't seem right,' the old boy muttered, shuffling off to attend to his duties. 'Makes me feel like a darned waiter.'

'Don't bother about Coonskin,' Sublette said, shrugging off his jailor's grunting after the old guy had departed. 'He loves to have something to grumble about. Let me fill you in on the duties of a deputy sheriff around here.'

Over the next couple of days, the lawman showed his new assistant around town, introducing him to all the local dignitaries. Sheriff Vince Sublette appeared efficient and well organized. When they were introduced, all the locals extolled him as a fine law officer. The local judge was exceedingly clear cut in his positive opinion of the sheriff's reputation. Any trouble that blew up was quickly squashed, the culprits locked up and transported to the territorial jail once each month if necessary.

'Finest law officer we've had in Bridger,' Judge Farthing gushed. 'Follow his advice, Deputy, and you won't go far wrong.' It certainly was a worthy endorsement.

Red nodded. Although somewhat obsequious, he

accepted at face value the veracity of universal acclaim regarding Sublette's handling of law enforcement. The problem of the missing deputies was not raised, and the new man had no desire to queer his pitch by exhibiting any unease he might have felt. Alerting the guilty parties, whomsoever they might be, that the new deputy posed a distinct threat, would be a foolish move. Better to display ignorance and investigate the issue in his own way, thus allaying any suspicion.

The next day found the two officers riding down the main street together. One particular official, however, caught Red's attention. 'Got me a pesky feeling that I've seen Mayor Gillan some place before,' he observed thoughtfully as they passed.

'Yep,' the sheriff agreed. 'He's gotten one of them faces, ain't he? Good man though.' The impression was cast to the back of Red's mind as he took heed of his duties. They included the usual things to ensure that a growing town prospered along lawful lines where everybody felt safe. Red gave no hint that he was already well acquainted with the job, having been a county sheriff himself in the eastern part of Wyoming territory, but under a different name.

CHAPTER TEN

DOWN AND OUT!

It was on the third day into the new job that Red accompanied the sheriff on a wider visit to the outlying regions of Caribou County. The route taken found them visiting the Lazy K ranch run by Charlotte Kimmel. 'Got me some personal business with this lady that takes priority over anything else,' Sublette declared with a sly wink. 'I intend inviting her to accompany me to next month's Saturday barn dance in town. We've been walking out, and I'm hoping to pop the question soon.'

When they arrived at the ranch, Red couldn't help but admire the sheriff's choice of lady friend. Her flowing locks of auburn hair waved freely in the breeze, and Mrs Kimmel was indeed a good-looking woman. Unlike many frontier wives, she had refused to be cowed by the hard work and tough existence that surviving on a frontier ranch demanded. This was an especially cogent observation when the new deputy discovered that she was a widow, and ran the ranch single-handedly with just the help of an old war veteran called Rooster Brown.

It was also patently clear that Vince Sublette had been exaggerating his relationship with the lady rancher, who clearly did not harbour a similar adulation. The sheriff was living in a dream world, and failed utterly to heed the cool response to his invitation. 'I might come along,' Charlotte languidly announced with an apathetic shrug. 'Depends on how the branding goes.'

'I thought we'd agreed that you would accompany me,' the sheriff pressed, still sitting atop his horse.

'You assumed too much, Vince. I'll make up my own mind whether or not to attend.' She made to move away, not even bothering to invite her visitors inside for some refreshment. Eager to get off the vexing topic of the sheriff's amorous intentions, Charlotte asked about the main thing currently on her mind: 'So have you managed to find those beeves that were rustled?'

Much to the woman's surprise, the sheriff was able to reassure her. 'The rustlers have been tried and found guilty, and are in the hoosegow awaiting transportation to the territorial prison. Unfortunately we haven't been able to find the stolen cattle.'

'Well, I'm pleased to know that justice has at last been done,' the woman said in a somewhat restrained tone. 'But that still don't mean I'm going to the dance. Thank you for telling me, but I have work to do, so I'll bid you good day.' She sashayed off, hips swaying provocatively without even asking the identity of the tall handsome stranger accompanying the sheriff. Had she done so, there might have been further questions posed when she learned that he was yet another new deputy. As it was, just like the desert wind that passeth by, this crucial predicament lay unresolved.

While this unsettling conversation was taking place, Red had moved away, not wishing to be a party to the wrangle. 'The sheriff is one mule-headed guy,' old Rooster sighed, shaking his head in a knowing way. 'Miss Charlotte won't be pushed around by anyone. And the more he presses her, the more she'll dig her heals in. My bet is that he's in for a rough ride.'

It was a red-faced lawman who silently rode away from the ranch. His deputy tagged along behind, allowing the disenchanted suitor to simmer down. No mention was made of the awkward meeting, Red Whyner merely commenting on the terrain and enquiring about the various landmarks. The impression he tried to convey was one of ignorance regarding the barely concealed put-down.

Initially uttering terse monosyllabic comments in response to his assistant's queries, Sublette eventually resumed his usual self-confident manner. Later in the day they arrived back in Bridger, with Red having spent most of his time on the trail thinking about the delectable Charlotte Kimmel. Women had come and gone in his life, many having been no more than passing fancies. Ruth Vender had been different, and he would always love her, no doubting that.

But a man needs female companionship. And he couldn't think of a more suitable woman to fill the empty void than Charlotte Kimmel. Maybe if'n he presented a more obliging image, she would give him a more positive reception than the obvious brush-off accorded to Sublette. But he would need to be subtle. The last thing he wanted was to antagonize the lawman. That would be as bad as, if not worse than expressing suspicions regarding the previous incumbents of his own position.

Perhaps some hunting on his day off would help to sort things out in his mind as to how best to handle both of the delicate situations. On suggesting the idea of a couple of days off to Vince Sublette, the sheriff immediately agreed, suggesting he take the following two days to investigate the northern part of Caribou County. 'It's mountain country with plenty of tree cover,' the lawman enthused. 'Ideal for hunting deer and wild turkey. Then you'll have experienced a full introduction to the territory we're meant to cover.'

While Vince went off to the saloon to silently drown his sorrows, Red stayed in the office trying to get to grips with the paperwork, the bane of every tin star's life. A check on the prisoners was revealing – and somewhat puzzling. This was the first jail he had come across where the cell inmates were supplied with enough trappings for a comfortable sojourn therein. There seemed to be plenty of tobacco, cards for gambling, together with good food. The only item missing was alcohol.

'Any chance of you slipping us a quart of hooch, Deputy?' It was Rufe Kegan who posed the request, much to the delight of his sidekicks. 'That old has-been out there is too darned mean.' Red gave the appeal a sour grimace, but offered no comment as he returned to the main office.

A further questioning of the turnkey induced the same response as previously. 'The judge claims to be an easy-going interpreter of legal details,' Coonskin exhaled noisily. 'He reckons being too harsh only serves to make felons more likely to break the law than mend their ways.' He lifted his hands as if to say '. . . it ain't my business to question official rulings'.

'All I do is look after the prisoners. But that don't mean to say I agree with letting the critters live the high life.'

It certainly was a conundrum to be mulled over on his forthcoming trip into the far-flung wilds of Caribou County. Before heading back to Ma Docherty's lodging house, Red asked to borrow one of the rifles in the wall rack. In the hurry to leave Laramie, he had clean forgotten that he had given his own rifle to Sam Vender, and the old Springfield was still lodged in his saddle boot. 'Take a couple if'n you want,' Radley concurred. 'That's what they're there for. Vince always uses his own. It's one of the latest Winchesters. He had it specially made in Casper.'

Back at the lodging house, Ma Docherty was more

101

than happy to furnish her guest with suitable grub to take on his trek. 'You look after yourself, fella,' she advised, a doleful expression clouding her wrinkled face. 'That's mighty wild country out yonder. Mountain lions, pumas and sneaky coyotes, all awaiting to fill their bellies with tasty human flesh.' The landlady was a fine cook, but her comment on enjoying the break left much to be desired.

Early next morning Red shrugged off the woman's gloomy forebodings and pointed his horse north. It felt good to be alone for a change, heading into the unknown. A couple of days free of responsibility would do him a world of good. By mid-morning he was entering the foothills of the Bitter Creek Range, the higher peaks towering above, coated in a permanent layer of white snow gleaming like icing on a cake. Bald-headed eagles floated overhead, circling on the warm thermals hunting out their own prey. A mesmerizing sight. In the distance, a herd of deer scooted off, sensing the approach of danger.

That night while Red Whyner was settling down beneath a blanket of twinkling stars, Judge Farthing was paying a visit to the jail. Coonskin was sitting in the sheriff's chair playing a game of patience. Displaying the agility of a mountain goat, the old turnkey immediately jumped to his feet. 'Don't get up on my account, Coonskin,' the rotund official generously declared. 'I'm only here to check that the prisoners are not causing you any bother.'

'Quiet as mice, your honour,' the old jailor

burbled bowing obsequiously to the high-ranking official. 'Fancy a cup of fresh coffee?'

'Don't mind if'n I do,' Farthing replied, taking a bottle out of his pocket. 'We might as well give it a bite while I'm here.' He poured a liberal slug into the jailor's cup. 'Reckon I'll pass with this stuff, though. Had my fair share already this evening.' He then left the bottle on the table. 'You help yourself, though. It'll help keep you warm through the long night ahead.'

Coonskin's eyes popped. A full bottle of top quality brandy all to himself. This was a dream come true. 'That's mighty generous of you, Judge,' he gushed.

'I always like to make sure all employees hired by the town are well looked after,' Farthing declared imperiously. They talked some more before the judge rose to his feet. 'I'll just check on the prisoners before getting on my way,' he said, moving across to the cell block. 'You stay here and enjoy some more of that brandy. Only the best for our revered turnkey.' The praise had old Coonskin drooling at the mouth.

After Farthing had left, Radley was all effusive praise for the official. 'Not many fellas of his rank would even pass the time of day with guys like me,' he muttered to himself. 'And he even left me that bottle of premium French brandy.' A leery smile flickered across the old trapper's crusty face as he poured himself another good measure. 'Yes indeed,' he murmured lying back in his chair, 'Judge Farthing is one fine gent.'

Ten minutes later the bottle was half empty, and the old trapper was bleary eyed and lolling in his seat. Another ten minutes and he was sleeping like a baby. With the moon high in the night sky, the rest of the town soon followed suit. Everything was quiet as the grave. Time for a shadowy figure to slip across the street and silently enter the jailhouse.

A quick check on the comatose turnkey was enough to raise a satisfied smile. The old soak was dead to the world, his regular snoring music to the ears. The newcomer slipped over to the cell block where he released the prisoners.

'OK, out you come, boys. And not a sound,' was the curt order. 'Old Coonskin don't know it, but he'll be your alibi come morning. Now follow me.' The mysterious liberator then led the released captives out the back door, where their horses were tethered and waiting. Each man's gunbelt was hanging over the saddle horn. 'You sure have this caper well organized,' Grizzly Frank remarked. 'I was beginning to think we'd be stuck in that cell 'til doomsday.'

'These things take time,' the head honcho declared. 'But your cut of the take will be worth the wait.' This was the first time Dodge and Behan had been involved in a robbery. But they had been given little choice in the matter. It was either that, or face a long spell in the pen. Both men were now hoping they had made the right decision.

'Now cut the chat and follow me.' The cagey gang boss was all eyes and ears to ensure they were not rumbled. 'We'll lead the horses round back of these storehouses so as not to make any noise,' he whispered. 'The last thing we want is to raise the alarm.'

Ten minutes later the leader of the six-man gang was satisfied they were well clear of the town. 'Mount up boys, we have to reach the north-bound trail from Green River if'n we're gonna stop the overnight payroll delivery to Fort Washakie. It should reach Muddy Mischief Gap by three in the morning, so we ain't gotten much time.'

Led by a man who clearly knew this country like the back of his hand, the outlaws made good time, maintaining a steady canter so as not to overstretch their mounts. After all, they needed to make this journey in reverse once the hold-up had been successfully completed. It was a clear night, which helped with navigation. But at no time during the three-hour trek did their leader go astray or his pace falter. Behan correctly surmised that he had done this before, as he remarked to his buddy.

'These other guys seem to be regulars as well,' Dodge added. 'Could be we're on to a good thing here if'n it works out.'

'I ain't so sure, Frank,' Behan countered nervously. 'What I can't figure is how we get out of that jail to spend the dough.'

Rufe Kegan had been listening in, and gave them the answer. 'The boss will have a prison wagon ready in a couple of days to take us to the territorial pen.' He hawked out a restrained laugh on seeing the gaping faces of the two nesters. 'Don't look so worried. We never make it to Sweetwater. Instead we disappear south over the border into Brown's Park and live the high life for a few months before the next job is planned. And nobody is any the wiser. It's a perfect racket. We've pulled it twice before. And it pays good as well.'

'What about the old turnkey,' Behan voiced uncertainly. 'Don't he smell a rat when the same guys keep appearing in his jail?'

Half Pint Lacey now took over validating the devious scheme. 'Half the time that old soak don't know what day it is. Give him a smell of hard liquor and he don't remember a thing come morning. A few months later and he wouldn't remember what his own mother looks like.' Laughs all round followed this mocking declaration.

'Quiet back there, you guys,' the boss hawked out. 'Muddy Mischief is just up ahead. We need to get prepared for the arrival of that wagon. It's due through there in fifteen minutes, so we've only just made the deadline. Those fellas always keep to a strict schedule.'

The shadowy profile of the distinctive notch in the rocky enclave appeared out of the gloom. And as if to welcome the gang of road agents, the silvery disc of the moon shuffled out from behind a cloud, casting a radiant glow over the terrain. The gang boss quickly deployed his men on both sides of the trail where it narrowed to pass through the gap. Half way through it forded a creek, which had given the pass its name.

'I sure hope this wagon is toting the twenty big

106

ones we've been promised,' Half Pint muttered to his sidekick.

'You worry too much,' Bull Braddock assured him, keeping an eye on the direction from which the stage coach would appear. 'Doesn't the bigwig who plans these jobs always come good? Only a guy in his position could suss out the most lucrative hauls to pull.'

'Cut the cackle, you guys,' Rufe Kegan snapped out. 'Looks like it's arrived. And spot on time as well.'

At that moment the boss's raised hand on the far side informed them that the coach had been spotted entering the far end of Muddy Mischief Gap. He had kept the two new men close by to make sure they toed the line: one false move from either of the nesters and it would be a bullet in the guts.

The steady rumble of the approaching coach had all six robbers tense and alert, clutching their weapons. Bandannas were pulled up to hide their faces. The moment of no return was at hand.

CHAPTER ELEVEN

NIGHTHAWKS ON THE PROD

Breaking cover, all six spurred out as the slowing wagon rumbled past. Guns blazing hot lead added to the thunderous drumbeat of hoofs. The driver and guard stood no chance against such a savage onslaught. Hit by three bullets the guard pitched over the side of the wagon, while the driver struggled desperately to restrain the panic-stricken team of four. But his attempts were hopeless, and a wheel struck a boulder as the wagon veered to one side of the narrow rift, breaking an axle. The sharp crack bounced off the surrounding rocks.

Totally out of control, the wagon slewed round, bucketing headlong into a huge rock. It crashed on its side and juddered to a halt, the wheels spinning furiously in protest. Whatever freight was being carried lay strewn across the trail. Even amidst the frenetic confusion, the driver still managed to draw his gun and pump out a couple of shots before joining his partner with the angels. He did, however, manage to wound one of the bandits.

Tom Behan clutched at his arm. 'I'm hit,' he called out.

'Cut the yammering,' his buddy snapped. 'You'll live. It's only a flesh wound. Let me tie your bandanna round it to stop the bleeding. We don't need them now.'

The rest of the gang ignored the injured man. All they were bothered about was locating that all-important strongbox carrying the much prized haul of twenty thousand in greenbacks. Boxes of general supplies bound for the fort were kicked aside as the outlaws urgently searched for the all-important loot.

Rufe Kegan was first to spot the iron-bound chest concealed beneath the upturned wagon. 'Here it is!' he shouted excitedly, dragging the heavy chest out into the open. All the outlaws gathered round. Even Behan had ceased his moaning as the boss man cocked his revolver and blasted the lock apart. All eyes greedily focused on the lid as it was slowly raised. A watery moon shone down, lighting up the interior of the chest.

And there it was. The army payroll that would now be put to much better use in Brown's Park once the pay-off had been made. Bundles of lovely notes tied up with string lying side by side. Gasps issued from dry throats at the sight of the rich haul. 'Suffering snakes!' Frank Dodge gurgled. 'I ain't never seen that much dough in my whole life before!' Eager hands fondled the stacks of paper money.'

'Stick with us, buddy,' Bull Braddock intoned, equally spellbound by the night's spoils, 'and this won't be the last time.'

'OK, boys!' the boss said, breaking into their one-track-minded concentration. 'We need to get out of here. It's a long ride back to Bridger, and we need to get you fellas safely re-established inside the jail afore that old drunk wakes up.' He made sure to pack their prize in his own saddle bags. 'Don't look so worried, Tom,' he scoffed at Behan's anxious look. 'It's only for a couple more days.' Then to the others. 'Let's eat dust, boys. You never know when somebody might happen along. It ain't just guys like us that are nighthawks.'

He was closer to the truth than he might have imagined. Camped over the far side of the nearby range of hills, Red Whyner had been jerked awake by a sound he could not at first place. He shook the mush from his head, thinking a night prowler such as a mountain lion was investigating his presence. His ears pricked up. It was certainly no animal intruder. The sharp crack of small arms fire, although distant, was now clearly audible. What in tarnation was going on out there in the wilds at this time of night?

The obvious conclusion that some kind of skul-duggery was afoot stirred his lethargic brain into action. He quickly broke camp. The sound of gunfire was coming from north of his current position. Speed was of the essence if'n he was to make his presence felt. But that was easier said than done in unfamiliar terrain at night. Serious injury to horse and rider was a possibility that could not be ignored. Consequently, he was forced to proceed with caution.

The thunder of hoofs alerted him as he crested a ridge. Peering over the rim he could see the vague outline of riders down below. And they were in a hurry, twisting and turning along a narrow draw towards where he was concealed. These critters were displaying all the attributes of robbers escaping from their recent attack. Red pushed his horse down the slope intending to waylay the suspects.

A cartridge was levered into the rifle obtained from the sheriff's office as he took up a challenging position. Two bullets were released, spurting sand up in front of the charging riders, forcing them to haul rein. 'This is a government law officer,' he rapped out making his presence known. 'And I'm ordering you men to identify yourselves and explain what all that shooting was about.'

The response was as expected. Sharp flashes of orange lanced his way, bullets ricocheting off nearby rocks. He quickly replied, despatching his own lethal comeback towards the orange flashes. But it had no effect. The leader of the band totally ignored the challenge, spurring his mount past the hidden rifleman as if he didn't give a hoot. The others followed behind, all blazing away at the threat to their

111

freedom, forcing Red to drop out of sight. In minutes they were past and disappearing into the gloom.

Red cursed, mounting up with the intention to follow them. But he was at a clear-cut disadvantage. They patently knew the country a sight better than him, and pursuit of a desperate foe at night would likely do more harm than good. Reluctantly he turned around and retraced the route followed by the gunmen.

What he found further along the canyon was expected, but no less harrowing. Cargo scattered across the wreckage of the ambush site was insignificant to the bodies of two dead men sprawled in the dust. Close by a ransacked strongbox told its own grim tale. Although used to sights like this, Red was nonetheless visibly shaken. It was always the same when death came a-calling in such a violent manner.

The bodies were manhandled into the bed of the wagon to keep them from being molested by wandering scavengers until they could be collected. He then released the horses from their traces. They would likely find their own way back to civilization. Little else could be done in the dark, so he retreated back to his campsite. No further thought could now be given to the planned hunting expedition.

More wood was placed on the fire to deter predators as he settled down. But what was troubling him most was the fact that, as a recognized sharpshooter with a rifle, his aim had been way off target. He gave the Winchester a thorough inspection in the flickering light from the fire. The action was tight and it appeared perfectly normal. Yet for some reason, the zeroing of the sights was set wrong. The conundrum was still taxing his brain when he finally fell asleep for the second time that night.

The robber gang meanwhile rode hell for leather back to Bridger. Only when the boss figured they had outfoxed the mysterious lawman did he signal a slower pace to conserve the energy of their flagging mounts. 'Who do you reckon that interfering turkey was?' Kegan asked. But nobody had an answer to that puzzle. 'At least we threw him off the scent. Any chance of a smoke break, boss?' Kegan added. 'The boys are all plum tuckered out after that long ride followed by the heist.'

'We keep riding,' was the curt response. 'You'll have plenty of time for rest and relaxation after the payoff. You guys have to be all tucked up in that nice cell block before Coonskin Radley wakes up.'

'I don't reckon there's much chance of that,' Kegan shot back. 'Judge Farthing will have made certain that woolly-headed old fool is still out long after we're back inside.'

'We ain't taking no chances,' the boss snapped. 'Especially now some nosey tin star will be snooping around.' He called to one of his regular guys to be back marker. 'Braddock, you hang back and make sure that jasper ain't sussed out which way we're headed.'

Fear of the law catching up found the gang silently eager to keep riding. It was only when Braddock reported that there was no sign of any pursuit that the mood relaxed. Grizzly Frank was the first to express his surprise that Judge Farthing was involved in the illegal venture. 'I'd never have guessed such a smart-assed dude like him would be mixed up in a sting like this,' he stated with a shake of the head. 'He sure is one cool jasper.'

'My betting is that he needs the dough for something more than just good whiskey,' Behan suggested. The two sodbusters had buried the hatchet since getting locked up together. 'Is he a gambler?' he asked the others.

'You've done hit the nail on the head there, pal,' Half-Pint confirmed with a laugh. 'He must owe Crackerjack Alty a small fortune the number of times I've see him stamping out of the Plainsman with his face so red it's near to bursting.'

'Don't any of you guys go bandying that around town, else you'll end up doing your full sentence in the pen,' the gang leader warned. 'The judge is mighty sensitive about his weakness for the pasteboards.' Nevertheless he couldn't resist a sly smirk of his own.

When they arrived back in Bridger, the false dawn was breaking over the eastern rim of the Steamboat Range. Time enough to ensure nobody was any the wiser to their clandestine activity. Even the night soil remover was still fast asleep in his pit. Rufe Kegan was placed in charge of bedding down the horses and

114

returning the guns to the armoury in the backroom of the jail. The head man then delivered the proceeds of the successful heist to the judge for safe keeping in his office.

Over at the jail, the perceived inmates re-entered their cells, quietly sniggering at the comatose figure of the turnkey who was still snoring. The empty bottle on the floor below where a hand hung down indicated it had been put to good use. 'That must have been a mighty strong knockout dose the judge put in the bottle,' Grizzly Frank observed.

'It served our purpose, that's for sure,' Kegan grunted. 'This old fool has given us a cast-iron alibi. Apart from that lawman almost upsetting the apple cart, that was a good night's work. All we need do now is await the final payout, then disappear over the border.'

'Brown's Park, here we come!' sniggered Half-Pint, much to the grinning satisfaction of his associates.

'Can't be soon enough for me,' grunted Braddock.

Another two hours passed before Radley struggled back into the land of the living. The early sun was streaming through the office window. He uttered a pained groan as the after-effects of the potent draught squeezed his head. All too soon he arrived at the obvious conclusion that he had drunk too much the previous night. Struggling to his feet, Coonskin staggered over to the window. Outside, folks were going about their normal business.

'Urrrgggggh!' he groaned, much to the delight of the prisoners, who were watching through the open door to the cell block. 'Never again. I must have slept right through the night.' Eager nods from the tittering inmates. Then a much more serious assumption wormed its way into the old timer's muddled thoughts. This wasn't the first time it had happened. Go on drinking like that and he knew his job would be on the line.

'How about some breakfast, old-timer,' Kegan shouted. 'You're late again. I'm gonna have to tell the sheriff about this poor attitude.' He struggled to keep the flippancy at bay as the turnkey dowsed his throbbing head in cold water. Without replying he lurched over to the door and left. The last thing he needed was having Vince Sublette learning about his weakness for the demon drink.

CHAPTER TWELVE

OUT IN THE OPEN

Next morning, Red set off back to Bridger. Much as he tried to pick up the trail of the fleeing brigands, he lost them crossing a bleak stretch of lava rock. They could be anywhere by now. Once again the mystery of that poorly zeroed rifle niggled in his mind. He stopped and removed the gun from the saddle boot and stepped down. Close up in daylight the sighting appeared normal; only a small error of adjustment would be needed to hinder the accuracy of the weapon.

So he decided to give it another try by aiming at a can of beans that he removed from his supplies and perched on a boulder some fifty yards distant; he then carefully sighted on to the target. After gently squeezing the trigger, the long gun bucked against his shoulder. In normal circumstances Red would have expected the can to leap into the air. Instead,

117

the bullet whined against a rock two feet to the right, proving beyond doubt that the gun was clearly off. No wonder he had not been able to bring down any of those robbers.

Either this was a mistake, or somebody had tampered with the weapon. Who would have done that? The obvious choice was the turnkey, whose job it was to clean and oil the guns ready for use. But old Coonskin just didn't seem the type to get involved in sabotage of that kind – and anyway, why would he want to? It didn't make sense. Red scratched his head in bafflement. Perhaps if'n he let the matter simmer awhile inside his head, the answer would be forthcoming. With that thought in mind, he made his way back to Bridger.

Back in town, Red headed straight for the jail. 'Where's Vince?' he enquired of the turnkey, who was looking a tad under the weather.

'He had to go out of town,' the old guy remarked. 'Something about a fencing dispute between sodbusters. They're getting more common since the influx of settlers following the Homestead Act. He'll tell you all about it when he returns. Did you have a good hunting trip?'

'I had to cut it short.' He went on to explain about the robbery. 'Can you organize it with the undertaker to go out to Muddy Mischief Gap and collect the bodies?'

'Sure thing, Red. I'll get on to it straightaway.' The last thing Radley wanted was anybody questioning his role as a competent jailor.

118

'How are the prisoners?' Red asked casually. 'They seem kinda quiet today.'

'That's cos I laid the law down.' The old jasper squared his narrow shoulders. 'Threatened 'em with no food at all if'n they didn't show me more respect.'

Red was impressed. 'It seems to have worked. I ain't so sure about the armoury in here though.' He pointed to the rack of long guns before handing over the suspect rifle. 'The sighting of this one is way off line. Maybe you should get the others checked out as well with the gunsmith.' He was carefully studying the old boy's reaction. If'n he was the guilty party, Radley sure was a good actor.

'I'll get on to it straightaway,' Coonskin again concurred, bobbing his head like a nodding donkey. 'Anything else you want me to do, just say the word.'

Red smiled. The old jasper seemed somewhat over eager to please. He shrugged it off as just his attempt to allay any notion that he was too old for the job. The fact that he had been totally blotto during the night guarding an empty jail was never suspected. 'I'm going off to get me some sleep. It's been a long night. So you're in charge.' That was something that pleased the turnkey no end.

It was past noon when he finally surfaced. Time enough for a visit to the Lazy K and the delectable Charlotte Kimmel. He would have to think up a suitable legal reason for calling on her. Just in case, like the sheriff, she turned him down as well. Surely he would have better luck than his boss's ham-fisted attempt to escort her to the next barn dance. It was a

119

challenge that effectively pushed the problem of the wayward rifle into the background.

And the nearer the budding suitor came to Lazy K land, the more nervous he became. This was the first woman he had shown any interest in since his beloved Ruth had passed away. From a steady canter, his pace had slowed to a walk. All kinds of formulaic lines buzzed around his head, each of which was dismissed as being either too forward or too bland. All too soon he caught sight of the ranch house.

Rooster Brown was in the yard mending a broken fence when he rode up. 'Mrs Kimmel in?' he asked, rather bluntly tempering the harsh tone to one of a more conciliatory tone. 'I need to speak with her about those steers that were rustled.'

'You found out what happened to them?' the ranch hand shot back. 'Those pesky rustlers admitted where they hid them?'

'Reckon it'd be best if'n I speak with the boss about that,' he said stepping down.

Rooster grunted, then slung a thumb towards the house. 'She's inside.' Then he turned and carried on with his interrupted task, much to the deputy's relief. Red gingerly knocked on the door, still trying to figure out how to broach the uppermost question on his mind. And it had nothing to do with stolen cattle. He had decided that a false excuse for his visit would be too obvious. Best to broach what was on his mind directly.

The lady herself answered the door. At least the caller was pleased to see that his visit was being received with a smile, and not the frown he had anticipated. Indeed she seemed positively pleased to see him. 'Come along inside, Deputy Whyner,' she breezed, holding the door open. An apron sprinkled with white flour harmonized perfectly with the smudges on her face. Altogether an entrancing sight.

Her somewhat homespun appearance made her all the more alluring. Red was instantly smitten. 'I h-hope I'm n-not intruding, ma'am,' he stuttered out an apology removing his hat. And feeling somewhat foolish. 'I was just p-passing and. . . .'

The wonderful picture in question appeared not to notice her guest's awkward manner. 'I'm glad you've called,' she butted in. 'I want to apologize for ignoring you on the last visit.'

Much to the lady's relief he brushed off her concern with a wry smile. 'Don't give it another thought, ma'am.'

'Well, you're in luck this time,' she gushed. 'I've just brewed a pot of fresh coffee. And as you can see, I've been baking.' The delicious smell of newly made fare wafted out from the kitchen. 'Perhaps you could be the first to sample my new recipe for cinnamon biscuits before old Rooster gets at them?'

A light-hearted bout of exchanged laughter gave the visitor hope that his reason for calling might well reap its reward. And sitting down with this vision in red gingham eating fresh biscuits was a good start. There was no denying he was famished. 'Nothing would give me greater pleasure, ma'am,' he assured her, meaning every word. He peered around the simple yet homely living room. Sepia photographs graced the bare wood walls, along with patterned Indian blankets. Most were of Charlotte and a man he took to be her late husband.

Noting his interest in the pictures, Charlotte offered enlightenment. 'My husband Dan was shot down by rustlers two years ago when he interrupted their thievery.' Her head drooped at the recollection. 'We had been married for five years. Nobody around here figured I'd carry on. But Dan had worked hard to make the ranch what it is today. And I had no intention of selling it off to some carpetbagger for a pittance.'

'Did they catch the skunks who shot him?' Red asked.

Charlotte shrugged. 'The lawman who was sheriff at the time was also shot while trying to make an arrest, and they escaped across the border into Brown's Park. That was the last I saw of my herd. It's been hard work building it up from scratch. I don't reckon I could have done it without the help of my foreman Rooster and young Chester. It was them who helped pull me through.' Her soulful expression faded as a much more mournful cast spread across the radiant countenance. 'And now they've been stolen again. Makes me wonder if'n it really is worth carrying on.'

'I reckon it is,' Red stressed, leaning in closer to lay emphasis on the appealing rancher's resilience. 'You've done a fine job of making this place a going concern. And rest assured, I'll do everything I can to find those beasts and return them to you.' It was a promise he dearly wanted to keep – but thus far was having little success of achieving. Whosoever was at the bottom of this chicanery was no tenderfoot, that was for sure.

Another thought then crossed Red's mind while sipping his coffee. 'So how long has Vince Sublette been your sheriff?'

Charlotte's face crinkled at the mention of her unwanted suitor. 'He and Judge Farthing arrived together about a year back after Sheriff Buff Granger retired.' Red's face remained inscrutable, but the news gave him food for thought. Those two had arrived together and clearly knew each other previously. It could mean something, or nothing.

His pensive expression was noticed by Charlotte. 'You appear to have something on your mind,' she broached.

That was certainly true. More than one thing, as well. Perhaps this the right moment to raise one of those issues, namely the dicey subject of the missing deputies. 'I hope I'll be around longer than the other guys who held this job.' He paused to assess her reaction. Sensing he had not overstepped the mark he continued. 'Have you any ideas as to what happened to them?'

The lady thought for a moment before answering. 'I've never really thought about it,' she admitted frowning. 'But now you've brought it up, it is kind of strange. The sheriff always passed them off as risks that go with the job. I can't see any reason to disagree with that conclusion.' Red nodded, figuring this was not the time to reveal any suspicions he might have harboured.

Over the interlude that followed, they talked about all manner of other things. Simple everyday stuff that Red had never took an interest in before. There was no denying that as well as lovely to behold, Charlotte Kimmel was easy to converse with. No mention was made of the highway robbery at Muddy Mischief Gap. Red did not want to spoil the moment of growing intimacy. Yet much as he tried summoning up the courage to pose the other issue on his mind, he always balked at the last moment.

What sort of weak-kneed milksop was he? It was only a dance. Girding himself, and with no further excuse to overstay his welcome, he was about to blurt out his request when a startling incident occurred that was to drive this affair of the heart into second place. Young Chester wandered into the room hoping to find that some cookies had been saved for him. In his hand was a sheet that looked awfully like a 'wanted' dodger.

'What's that you have there, Ches?' his mother asked. The boy showed her the sheet on which was boldly written the word 'WANTED'. Underneath was a reward of $5,000, together with a description of the villain and his misdemeanours. The boy had been adding his own artistic endeavours to the pen drawing of none other than . . . the visitor gulped . . . *Skinny Jim Fresno*.

'Where did you get that?' Red snapped, grabbing

hold of the paper. He instantly regretted his harsh action. 'Sorry to scare you, boy, but I've been after this critter for some time. He killed a buddy of mine in Colorado.'

'It was p-pinned up to a t-tree back along the trail,' the boy stammered. 'I didn't do wrong, did I?'

Red ruffled the boy's hair. 'Of course not, son. It was a mighty big shock to see this varmint's ugly mush again. I thought I'd lost him for good. Now I ain't so sure after seeing this.' His eyes narrowed as he studied the amended depiction. The clean-shaven angular face of Fresno had been transformed by the addition of a curled moustache and beard. 'So that's where I've seen you before, Mister Mayor,' he muttered under his breath. 'I'm wondering if'n this is just a twist of fate – or is there something more sinister at work here?'

An explanation of this unexpected revelation was clearly needed to assuage the concern etched on Charlotte Kimmel's face. Perhaps this was the moment to reveal his true identity and the reason for his presence here in Caribou County, and Bridger in particular. But could he trust this woman to support him – and more importantly, keep quiet about what he was about to expose? For what seemed like a month of Sundays, silence enfolded the domestic scene. A palpable tension had suddenly clouded the easy-going tête-à-tête. Each of the cast members sat still, waiting for the other to say something.

It was Charlotte who broke the impasse. It was as if she could read the new deputy's mind. 'If'n you have something to say about this . . .' she observed in a low yet decisive drawl, jabbing a finger at the wanted poster '. . . rest assured that any disclosure will remain within these walls. Isn't that right, Chester?' An intense look was fastened on to her son.

'It sure is, Ma,' the boy concurred vigorously, nodding his head. This was playing out just like the dime novels he avidly devoured. But now it was real life. Could this tall stranger be a bounty hunter after a wanted outlaw? 'Honestly, sir,' he burbled. 'You can trust me and Ma to keep our mouths shut.'

'That's all I wanted to hear,' the enigmatic visitor said. 'To start with then, my name ain't Red Whyner. . . .' A gasp from the boy was matched by his mother's fluttering eyebrows raised in surprise. 'It's Drew Henry. Same letters, different name. And I'm a field agent with the Bureau of Advanced Detection based in Laramie.'

'Gee wizz!' exclaimed Chester, his mouth hanging open. 'Hear that, Ma? A real BAD guy, and here in our house!' Along with other Western heroes, their adventures, although much exaggerated, were the reading fodder of innumerable imaginative young minds throughout the frontier territories.

'Give the man a chance to get his breath, Ches,' his mother cautioned, not wishing her son to become too overexcited. A cool head was clearly needed to absorb what was about to be revealed. 'Perhaps we should all calm down a tad and catch our breaths.' She stood up. 'I'll make us a fresh pot of coffee. And maybe add a drop of the hard stuff to it. I have the feeling that both of us are going to need a stiffener.'

While Charlotte was out of the room, Drew revealed to his young listener some of the less grisly episodes in which he had been engaged as a BAD agent. When they were settled once again he began his explanation. 'So it's like this. . . .'

Once the startling events had been explained, silence once again descended as the revelations sunk in. 'So what do you intend doing now?' Charlotte asked. 'I can't believe that a man like Cyrus Gillan is involved in criminal activity. He's a successful businessman in his own right, and deacon of the church. Only those held in the highest respect would ever be elected to such an honourable position as Mayor.'

She had put forward a telling case in Gillan's favour. But Drew was still not fully convinced. 'Well, this picture young Chester has brought home and drawn over is a dead ringer for the guy,' he stressed, waving the dodger. 'There's too much of a likeness for it to be a fluke of nature. Maybe Jim Fresno is his twin brother. Whatever the truth, I mean to suss it out.' He now adjudged it the right time to leave the ranch. The original reason for his visit would have to be put on hold. This matter was too vital for any distraction. And it needed tackling without delay. 'Could you give me directions to the mayor's home?'

CHAPTER THIRTEEN

TAINTED SILVER

Night had fallen before Drew came in sight of the screen of trees behind which the mayor's house was located. It lay a mile off the main trail back to Bridger, with no other properties around. An owl hooted close by, adding its haunting lament to the tension. Overhead the dying sun still managed to cast a gentle glow over the western backdrop of mountains, etching them in stark relief. Drew couldn't help feeling that the 'much esteemed' official had done very well for himself. But was his success based on personal endeavour, or illicit gain?

That was a question he intended uncovering before daylight – though he had given no thought as to how he might proceed. Should he challenge the official by showing him the poster? Or maybe the whole mayoral thing was just a charade to hide his nefarious dealings? Drew concealed himself in the

128

shadows overlooking the house, still unsure how to handle the matter. Ten minutes passed before he finally decided to challenge the official head on.

But emerging from cover, the decision was taken out of his hands by the steady drum of hoofbeats approaching the house, causing him to pull back just in time: moments later a shadowy figure cautiously drew near. The mysterious visitor peered around nervously before approaching the front door. Light from the house revealed the face of none other than Skinny Jim Fresno himself.

Drew swallowed. So he had been right in his assumption: the two men were related. Fresno knocked on the door, which was opened by the mayor. The official's surprise was palpable at the obviously unanticipated visit. 'What in thunder are you doing here?' he rasped, looking round to make sure nobody else was in the vicinity. He failed to spot the well concealed watcher in the trees. 'Didn't you get the message the last time? There'll be no more handouts from me. You might be my brother, but I won't take the risk of having you drag our good name down in the mud.'

'Quit your belly-aching, big shot,' Fresno griped. 'Ain't I always kept my mouth shut before? Let me in and I'll tell you what I want. Then you'll never have to set eyes on me again. And that's a promise, brother.'

'Say what you've come for out here,' Gillan replied, barring his brother from entering the house. 'The only decent thing you did in embracing the

129

lawless life was to change your name. I'll give you a grub stake and some food. Then we're quits. I've established an honest, god-fearing life here, and I don't want you spoiling it. '

'All high and mighty as usual,' sneered Fresno. 'Well, here's what you're gonna do.' From his position, Drew could easily hear what was being said. Both men were alike in their physical appearance, but totally diverse in character. Fresno pulled an envelope out of his pocket and handed it to his brother. 'I want you to deliver this message first thing in the morning.' He jabbed a finger at the name written on the front. 'This guy will do exactly as I've written inside, you can bet on it.'

The mayor was sceptical, his tone scornful. 'What business could you possibly have with a man like that?'

Fresno was evasive. 'Let's just say that I can pull the rug from under the scheming operation he's running here.'

'What are you talking about?'

'Best you don't know, Cy. Just deliver the note. Stick it under his door before anybody's up and about, then disappear. That way you have no connection with what I want from him, and the precious family name remains untarnished. You got that? You'll be protected from any comeback, and you won't have to set eyes on me again.'

'I don't want you causing any harm to people I have to deal with, Jim,' the mayor warned. 'Promise me this letter does not involve any shooting.'

A harsh guffaw echoed around the perimeter of the house. 'That's the last thing I want. What I *do* want is this guy to set me up for a life on easy street. And he'll do it, too, if'n he's any sense. Last thing that fella wants is me raising Cain about this business.'

'What kind of business are you talking about?' Gillan pressed uneasily.

'Like I said before, you're safer being kept in ignorance, brother.' Fresno was giving nothing away. 'Just deliver the note to set up a meeting with the guy and let me handle the rest. Once I'm out of here, you can do whatever you feel is best. Until then, keep your trap shut.' The biting retort was tempered by an offered hand. 'It's for your own good.' Reluctantly Gillan accepted the conciliatory gesture. 'This is the final parting of the ways, Cy.' There was a note of regret in his voice. 'But that's the way it has to be, for both our sakes.'

And with that he departed, leaving his brother scratching his head in bewilderment.

Drew had been hanging on every word uttered between the Gillan brothers. Clarity regarding the mayor's innocence of any wrongdoing was masked by his brother's sinister summons to an unknown person in Bridger. And what sort of funny business was this guy involved in? Maybe it had something to do with the disappearance of the deputies he had come to investigate. The only way to discover the truth was to stick close to Fresno and witness his meeting, whenever that might be. In all likelihood it

131

would be the next day. The outlaw would have no
wish to linger and risk being caught.

A clear night with the moon bathing the terrain in
an ethereal radiance provided enough light for Drew
to track his quarry without being spotted. So confident was the outlaw of his position that he made no
effort to conceal where he was camped out. After a
half-hour, Fresno disappeared from view along a
narrow draw. Drew slowed to a walk, not wishing to
compromise his clandestine undercover action.

Well off the beaten trail, the glow from a fire
informed him of his quarry's night camp. The cocky
braggart had even kept it burning. Drew dismounted
a hundred yards short of the camp, and led his horse
off into the tree cover. There he tied it up and cautiously approached the camp. Fresno had a pot of
coffee and some food waiting to be reheated. Drew,
on the other hand, had to remain alert, not knowing
when Fresno would make his move.

It was going to be a long night. He gave thanks to
the heavens that a rainstorm brewing over the
Rockies had trundled north. Luckily he had his own
camping gear ready to hand, and managed to estab-
lish a reasonably comfortable watch overlooking his
quarry's own camp. Instead of hot food, however,
Drew would have to make do with jerked beef, cold
biscuits and water.

During the early hours the sentinel inevitably succumbed to the gentle persuasion of Orpheus and fell
asleep. He was jerked awake by a wandering coyote
sniffing at his smelly feet. The animal scampered

away on being detected. Dawn had already broken over the scalloped ramparts to the east. Hurriedly crawling across to the rim of his hideout, Drew anxiously surveyed his adversary's camp. A visible sigh of relief issued from tightly clenched teeth on seeing the huddled form beside the dying embers of the fire.

A few hours' sleep had worked wonders, however, and with the new day pressing onwards, Drew Henry was equally ready for what it might bring. Fresno surfaced a half-hour later, and much to the spectator's anguish, stoked up the fire to brew some fresh coffee. Even at that range, the luxurious smell was difficult to bear. Water and more jerky came a poor second.

Mumbled imprecations urged the outlaw to hurry up and get on the move: the sooner this business was uncovered and hopefully resolved, the better. At least Drew had the advantage of surprise on his side. After what seemed like a deliberate piece of loitering, the outlaw doused the fire with the grounds of his coffee pot, and walked across to where his horse was tethered in the brush. At last, muttered the irritated watcher.

But Drew's blood boiled when he saw the woebegone condition of the much prized Barbary stolen by Fresno following their last clash. He could have plugged the bastard there and then for driving the horse into the ground in the way he had. But he held his temper in check. It was now a case of discreet tracking, for which Drew Henry was renowned.

As Fresno harboured no suspicion of being followed, he proved an easy mark, leaving numerous clear signs as to his route. An hour later he halted in a narrow gulch known locally as Dead Man's Gate. Was this an ominous precursor of what was to come? Only time would tell. And the tracker didn't have long to wait.

Ten minutes of tense prowling followed before the rotund figure of none other than Judge Malachi Farthing appeared at the far end of the narrow ravine. Drew had positioned himself at the perfect site overlooking the gruesomely named meeting place. And there he sat, silently studying the approaching official, who had evidently been curtly summoned by this lawless brigand. The judge pulled up short and dismounted. Slowly he approached the waiting man, a concerned look etched across his fat visage.

Farthing huffed, summoning up all his official bluster to demand an explanation. 'What is the meaning of this message fetching me out to this godforsaken place?' He waved the missive in the air. 'There is nothing in here to explain what you want!'

An ugly gurgle meant to be a laugh rumbled in Jim Gillan's – alias Fresno's – throat. 'Guess you don't recognize me, eh, Judge?'

The official sniffed imperiously. 'Am I meant to?'

'It was over four years since,' Fresno declared, shaking a fist in the arrogant toad's face. 'And you were the brains behind that jailbreak scam in Denver, when you drugged the turnkey same as you did here,

I'll bet. I was one of the dupes who paid the price for your little scheme going wrong. Ten years in the pen we got saddled with. Unlucky for you I broke out. So here I am now, still alive and kicking. But it'll be you who gets kicked if'n you don't play ball.'

Farthing attempted to play the innocent by denying all knowledge of any underhanded chicanery. 'I don't know what you're talking about, mister,' he blustered, puffing out his silken vest. 'Accusing a legally appointed judge of criminal behaviour is a serious offence and will send you back to jail in double-quick time. I'll make sure of that. And this time I'll have you in chains.'

The supercilious leer coating Fresno's face indicated he was in no way intimidated. 'Don't try denying it. You're as guilty as we were, more so if'n truth be told. That caper must have netted you a handsome profit while me and the boys did all the hard work.'

The ashen look on the judge's face told its own story. He remembered all right. He also recalled that it had been a close shave, and no mistake. He and his partner in crime had gotten out by the skin of their teeth, leaving their collaborators, men like Skinny Jim Fresno, to take the rap. 'I can see now that you remember when that last hold-up went all wrong. And it was guys like me that shouldered all the blame.' He jabbed a finger in his chest. 'Well, I'm here to put things right. You're in cahoots with another bunch of poor saps now, and pulling the same stunt here in Wyoming.'

135

Thick eyebrows met on the judge's worried face as he considered the implications of this man's sudden and unwelcome appearance. 'How did you learn about this?' he enquired.

'One of the owlhooters who left the gang after your last heist spilled the beans over a few drinks when I was passing through Baggs.' Fresno smiled. He was enjoying his dominance over this pompous dumbcluck. 'Remember Little Billy Scout?' The intake of breath from the judge was enough to see Fresno continuing with his story. 'Yeh,' he sneered. 'I thought you would. He was heading up north into Montana to spend his ill-gotten gains. It got me to thinking how I could cash in on your lucrative scam down here in Caribou County.'

The judge was fidgeting, unsure how to respond. 'So what do you want?' he said after due consideration. 'If'n it's a cosy place in the jailhouse on our next job, I'm sure that can be arranged.'

A blunt interruption effectively squashed that notion. An overbearing snort greeted the surly offer. 'No way am I going to take up residence in a jailhouse. Never again,' he snarled, stepping forward in a threatening manner. The sudden move caused Farthing to jump back. Fresno wagged a menacing finger in the judge's scared face. 'I want fifty thousand in greenbacks, plus a fresh horse. Take it or leave it. But think hard on what I could do should the answer be a shake of the head.'

Drew was avidly listening to all that was being said. Now he fully understood the bleak nature of the crooked game being played in Bridger, with this fat dude the brains behind the whole seedy business. What he did not suspect, so intent was he on listening in, was that another watcher was hidden amongst the dense tree cover enclosing Dead Man's Gate.

'You must be mad if'n you think I'll hand over that amount of dough. . . .'

'You'd better, Judge,' Fresno butted in with a rabid growl, 'or the curtain falls. You obviously don't know it, but I've gotten influential contacts around here that will blow your scheme apart. All I have to do is say the word.'

Farthing huffed and puffed. 'You're bluffing. Who in tarnation does a lowlife like you know around here?'

'That ain't none of your business.' Even a hardened villain like Skinny Jim Fresno had no wish to tar his own kin with the name of a wanted outlaw.

'It don't matter none, anyway,' the judge sneered unmoved by the threats made. 'The game's up for you, mister. Nobody tries to dry gulch me and gets away with it!' Judge Farthing then pulled back, raising his hand as he looked up towards the line of trees on his right. 'OK, Vince, cut the bastard down to size.'

Too late Drew was made savvy to the truth.

The blast from a shotgun rocked the secluded location. The load from a single barrel struck the outlaw on the shoulder spinning him around. 'Aaaaaaargh!' Fresno cried out staggering back. Desperation laid its icy hand on the traumatized features as his stunned brain attempted to figure out what had gone wrong.

137

CHAPTER FOURTEEN

A GATE WELL NAMED

That was the moment Vince Sublette revealed himself on the same side of the gulch as Drew but some fifty yards distant. Drew pulled back under cover. He was shaken to the core to discover that his boss was in cahoots with the devious attorney. Gaping eyes fastened onto the hunched figure as he emerged from cover and carefully made his way down to where his trembling associate was panting as he stared at the injured man.

Although badly hit, Fresno still retained enough strength to draw his revolver. A second crash was enough to finish the uneven contest. A reflex jerk from the wounded man's trigger finger pumped a

138

couple of bullets into the sand before he succumbed to the Devil's handshake. Farthing had reason to breathe much harder when the second barrel finished the job. So close was the blast that it caused the body to jump in the air scaring the Judge half to death. Farthing's mouth flapped like a wind-blown door.

Although instigated by the pompous advocate, this sudden outburst of violence saw him bleating in terror as he lurched away from the bloody mess. He was a planner, a schemer at heart. All the heavy stuff was always left for others to carry out. Gunplay always left him cold, especially when he was in the firing line. His ashen face, twitching with fear, elicited a mocking scowl from his accomplice.

'Pull yourself together. He won't be causing us no trouble any more. The brash chiseller figured he had all angles covered,' Sublette grunted, toeing the body to ensure his victim was dead. 'What he forgot was that you and me are pards. Only a fool would think you would meet him alone in this out-of-the-way spot.'

Sublette nonchalantly lowered the shotgun, satisfied that a problem had been squashed. 'What you worried for?' he scoffed, throwing a leer of contempt at the angst-ridden frown creasing his pard's blotched face. 'We're in the clear. Once I set off for Sweetwater with the boys and allow them to somehow disappear, I'll be able to think of a way to rid myself of that new deputy. I don't trust the critter. He's a mite too keen for my liking, just like that kid McVay.'

139

'If'n this guy Fresno knew about our scheme, others are likely too as well,' the twitchy gavel-basher bleated. 'I reckon it's time we cut and run, Vince. We should head for Brown's Park straightaway and lie low until the heat dies down. There's enough dough in my safe to keep us in clover for a good long spell. Then we can start up again some place new where we ain't known.' He paused, stumbling about like a lost dog. 'You get rid of Whyner now and the authorities are gonna become mighty suspicious about so many deputies ending up on the undertaker's slab.'

'You're right there, Judge,' a terse voice barked from the far side of the clearing. Drew had heard all he needed to. 'The law has already become involved. And they've sent me to find out what's been going on around here.' Drew then made his presence known. Stepping out into the open, he held his revolver steady.

Both of the guilty parties froze before whirling round to face their accuser. So startled were they that any retaliatory action was rendered ineffective.

'Now I know for certain it was you two that planned and executed those robberies and rustled those steers.' He had no proof of the accusation but their guilt-ridden faces told him he had hit the nail on the head. 'Quite an operation you had going here. You sure had everybody fooled, me included. Luckily an artistic kid with a pencil opened the door for me.' The blank looks made him laugh out loud. 'You'll hear about it at the trial.' Without waiting for any response he hurried on, his follow-up rasp aimed

140

at the crooked sheriff. 'Is that how you finished off my buddy, Angus McVay, and those other deputies? With a shotgun from cover?'

Farthing was trembling with fear. But Sublette was made of sterner stuff. He recovered his wits, quickly denying any such charge. 'I never killed McVay,' he protested. 'It was me that tried to save him from those rustlers. But I was too late.'

'So what happened?' Drew snapped, drilling the squirming braggart with a beady eye. 'You tell me.'

'His right hand had drawn a gun, but the skunk let him have it with a shotgun.' His voice rose to emphasize he was telling the truth. 'I tried to help, but there were too many of them. And poor Angus paid the price. You gotta believe me, Red. That's how it was.' The sturdy flamboyant lawman had taken the role of a pleading puppet.

'I believe you all right, Sublette.' An evil grin lacking any hint of levity split the handsome visage. Then it slipped, replaced by a hard leer. 'I believe you're a dirty liar. Angus was left-handed. He would never have deliberately used his right hand in such a situation. And another thing. It was me that interrupted your brazen killing spree at Muddy Mischief Gap. It's only now that I've come to realize that you were the leader of that bunch. I'm sure in my own mind that Coonskin didn't tamper with those rifles. So it could only have been you.'

Sublette's poignant silence gave him the answer.

'From what Fresno admitted it was also you that freed the rest of your gang from the jail while poor

141

old Coonskin was out cold from a knockout potion fed by the judge here.' He then turned to address the burbling adjudicator. 'Ain't that so, your honour?'

'Don't say a word, Farthing!' Sublette rasped. All deference to the guy's status had dissolved. 'It's only his word against ours. This guy is just some nosey critter trying to get revenge for his pal's death and shift the blame on to us. Nobody will believe him against the testimony of a highly respected territorial judge.'

'Some nosey critter you think, eh?' Drew snarled, gritting his teeth. Nothing would give him more pleasure than rubbing this rat's face in the dirt. But he needed to maintain an even composure. Keeping his gun level, he then removed the revered badge from his vest pocket and pinned it on the lapel in place of the lowly deputy's star. Tapping it, he then revealed who he really was, as the two conspirators quickly got the message. 'The BAD organization has had you in its sights since those deputies went missing. And if'n you rearrange the letters of my name, guess what emerges?'

Farthing realized the significance first. His face flushed, rubbery lips quivering with trepidation. 'You're Drew Henry?' he burbled.

'The very same, buster.' A grin of satisfaction melded with the glitter of triumph in his eyes. Now it was Sublette's turn to swallow nervously. Every lawman in Wyoming territory and beyond was privy to the august name of the highly respected, and in their case much feared, BAD boy. 'I'm placing you

142

skunks under arrest. I've enough evidence here to see you both swinging from a rope's end.'

That was too much for Farthing. He broke down, pleading his innocence in a fearful bout of snivelling. 'I admit to breaking the law, but I had nothing to do with any killings. That was Sublette's doing. It was he who insisted they had to be rubbed out. I tried to stop him. But he wouldn't listen to sense.'

'You double-crossing louse!' the bent lawman snarled as the blubbing official stumbled towards Drew, pleading for mercy.

That was the moment Sublette saw his chance. And he took it by grabbing the cringing weasel round the neck. His own revolver was palmed and jammed into the turncoat's neck. 'I'm pulling out of here,' he snarled. 'And this bag of wind is my insurance policy. I'm sure an upright guy like you, Henry, won't deliberately shoot a man in cold blood. That ain't in your book of rules, is it?' He hawked out a chilling guffaw. 'Now toss that gun over here. I wouldn't want you getting any bright ideas to try and stop me.'

Drew cursed his ill fortune, but refused to abandon the revolver, which remained rock steady in his hand. 'Not a chance, Sublette,' he snapped, backing off. 'Do that and you'll gun me down for sure. Unlike ruthless skunks like you, Drew Henry still has scruples.' He turned sideways offering a reduced target while backing off towards the tree cover.

'One false move remember and the judge here

143

gets it,' Sublette threatened.

Drew merely hawked out a brittle guffaw. 'I don't think so.' Although his adversary was concealed, Sublette, he knew, was well aware that if he responded with gunfire, Farthing would likely be hit. And there was no chance of him holding up the dead weight of the rotund gavel-basher.

It was a Mexican stand-off. The disgraced sheriff was in a precarious position. So he started to back away towards where he had hidden his horse. Drew made to follow, but the blunt-edged threat of violence forced him to remain where he was. 'Try following me and it'll be this backstabber's blood on your hands.' The spurious lawman's threat was enough to enable him to escape.

Yet still Drew attempted to pour cold water on his shallow evasion tactics. 'You won't get away, fella,' he called after the retreating figures. 'That guy will slow you down, so I'll be dogging your trail. And when you get tired I'll make my move.'

Straightaway, Drew knew he had said the wrong thing. A ruthless predator like Sublette would have no compunction in gunning down his partner once out of immediate danger. Then the gloves would be off. One against one. That piece of logic struck home with a vengeance. Moments later two shots rang out. The abruptness of the retaliation made Drew fully aware that his warning had been mercilessly heeded. Galloping hoofbeats indicated the fugitive sheriff had abandoned his dead hostage and was making his getaway unhindered.

Blood drained from the BAD agent's face as he hurried through the trees, fearing the worst. And so it proved. Judge Farthing had a bullet in his head. But worse as far as Drew was concerned, Sublette had taken Fresno's hardier Barbary and shot both his own and the judge's mount.

CHAPTER FIFTEEN

WRONG PLACE, WRONG TIME

A distant bout of cynical laughter from the escaping desperado filtered through the trees, knowing his nemesis had been cast afoot. All he needed to do now was get back to Bridger and break into the safe where all the dough from the recent robbery was sitting. Then he would leave the territory and head for Brown's Park. Alone. With Henry cast afoot, there would be nobody to hinder his flight. Easy as pie. Unfortunately he had forgotten about Drew's own horse.

In the dim light of early morning, however, the crooked lawman had failed to spot the poor condition of the once fine animal, so anxious was he to get clear of the Dead Man's Gate. But even a hardy cayuse like the Barbary needs to be looked after, and

Fresno had failed miserably in that respect. Only when Sublette tried pushing the horse to a gallop did he realize his critical error.

No amount of cussing and vicious spurring could induce more speed from the wretched animal. Cursing his folly brought no relief from the dire predicament. No wonder Fresno had wanted another horse. This one was fit only for the glue factory. He would be lucky to even reach Bridger except at walking pace. But the brigand had not achieved success in his devious chicanery by idly accepting his plight. The scheming mind immediately set to work figuring out a plan of action.

He soon arrived at the obvious answer. The Lazy K was the nearest spread where he could exchange this broken-down nag for a decent mount. But that could not be done by just riding in and making his request. Too many awkward questions would be forthcoming from that cantankerous old has-been Rooster Brown. He would need to do it on the sly.

Sublette approached the ranch with extreme care. The last thing he needed was having to explain his presence to Charlotte Kimmel or the hired help. Time hung heavy as he impatiently searched for any sign of movement. Just when it seemed OK to approach the barn where the horses were stabled, a movement at the front of the ranch house made the watcher back off. It was Charlotte.

Even in this dire moment when escape from the real law was of the essence, the bogus sheriff couldn't fail to admire the woman's lithe form as she sashayed

147

over to water her vegetable garden. A lascivious tongue licked at his upper lip, drooling eyes pouring over the woman's sensuous yet totally innocent movements. He was almost tempted to linger and have his way with her. If'n he hadn't been in so much of a hurry, he certainly would have. That would sure teach her that refusing his advances was a serious mistake.

But survival and being able to enjoy his ill-gotten gains in the safety of Brown's Park had to take priority over any lustful satisfaction. He waited for the woman to finish her task and go back inside the house. Old Rooster was nowhere to be seen, nor was that cocksure brat of a son, either. This was the moment to make his move. Leaving the Barbary tethered to a tree, he hustled across the open sward on the blind side of the house towards the barn. All the while his nervous eyes were constantly searching for any unwanted interference.

Slipping inside the barn he quickly found a suitable horse and saddled up. A leer of satisfaction cracked the stoic demeanour as he made to mount up. 'What the heck are you doing in here, Sheriff?' The sharp retort had come from the startled lips of Rooster Brown. The foreman had been forking hay into the stalls at the rear of the barn when he heard some unexplained noises at the far end.

Sublette was fleetingly stunned by this sudden hindrance to his plans. He stuttered out a feeble excuse. 'My horse went lame back up the trail and I had to leave him.'

A cynical grunt greeted the weak excuse. 'That's as may be, but it's normal practice to ask the owner of the spread if'n you want to borrow a horse. I figured a lawman would know that.' Rooster scratched his bald pate. He was not one to hold back when he felt somebody was overstepping their authority. 'I'd better go speak to the boss about this. She'll want to know.' The old guy's brow furrowed in puzzlement. There was something not quite right here. The guy was acting much too furtive.

Bringing Charlotte Kimmel in on the exchange was the last thing Sublette wanted. This old coot was becoming a boil on his ass that needed lancing. A gun shot was out of the question as it would immediately alert Charlotte that trouble had come a-calling. He sidled over to where Rooster had left his pitchfork. The foreman had turned away to go seek out his boss. 'I don't reckon that's a good idea,' Sublette hissed, grasping hold of the implement. As the oblivious cowpoke paused and turned round to respond, his assailant rushed forwards, driving the lethal twin-pronged implement into Rooster's stomach.

A choking gurgle issued from the open mouth as the poor guy hung suspended where the fork had pinned him to a stall. A stream of blood spurted forth, spattering the attacker. Utter shock spread across the injured man's twitching face. But he wasn't dead. Sublette let out a growled curse and withdrew a large bowie knife from his belt, and without a second thought he rammed it into Rooster's heaving chest, effectively finishing the job.

'I didn't want to do that, you crazy galoot,' he muttered to the dead body after removing the knife and wiping it clean on the foreman's leg. 'You ought to have kept your nose out.' No further time was wasted on idle speculation of what his action might precipitate. He needed to get clear and head for Bridger pronto. But care was still needed to leave the ranch unseen. After leading the fresh horse out the back of the barn, he walked it away from the house before mounting up.

He could only hope that Charlotte did not go looking for her foreman in the immediate future. Every second now counted to give him the chance of escaping Caribou County and Wyoming undetected.

Drew Henry could not help lamenting his ignominious plight. His own horse had been bitten by a rattler and he had been forced to dispose of it with a bullet in the brain. Cast afoot miles from the nearest habitation. Could his luck have been any worse? And how could he not have suspected the devious sheriff of duplicity? All the clues had pointed in his direction.

The crooked judge was guilty of playing a double hand, but he was now dead due to Drew Henry's inept handling of the tricky situation. And having made a mug of him, Sublette was now out of reach. By the time he managed to borrow a horse, the rat would have disappeared over the horizon, well on his way to enjoying the dubious delights of Brown's Park.

After this calamitous fiasco, retirement was a foregone conclusion. He would not be able to hold his

150

head up in BAD company ever again.

He had been walking in the general direction of the Lazy K for upwards of an hour when a rider appeared on the horizon. His heart gave a lurch of hope. Maybe all was not yet lost. As the figure approached Drew heaved a sigh of relief. It was none other than Chester Kimmel. The boy was equally surprised to see his hero reduced to foot-slogging.

Before the boy could voice the obvious query on his lips, Drew held up a hand. 'This is no time for explanations, Chester. I need a horse, and quick, if'n I am going to catch the skunk who's been killing all those other deputies.'

The boy nodded, dumbfounded at finding the BAD agent on foot and needing his help. 'Climb up behind,' he said, 'Tumbleweed here is the fastest horse in the county. Carrying double won't stretch him one jot.'

Drew swung up on to the black stallion. The boy's faith in his horse was well gauged. The miles flew by and in no time they reached the Lazy K, shuddering to a crazy halt outside the ranch house. Charlotte was anxiously waiting for them on the veranda having heard the pounding of hoof beats from afar.

'What's gone wrong?' she urgently enquired as Drew slid off Tumbleweed's foam-flecked back. 'Did your confrontation with Cyrus not go to plan?'

'Something like that, ma'am,' he replied somewhat sharply. 'I ain't gotten time to explain now. I need to borrow a fast horse. All I can say at the moment is that our good sheriff of Bridger is a double-dealing skunk and a ruthless killer. I'll tell you about it after I've scotched the rat's bid to escape justice.'

Charlotte gasped on hearing this barely credible revelation. But Drew Henry's brusque demeanour was enough for her to know better than to question his motives for such a momentous accusation. 'We'll go over to see what Rooster has available,' she averred stepping down and hustling across to the barn. 'He always keeps a few horses fresh in case they're needed in a hurry.'

Drew followed, eager to get on his way. He had already figured out that Sublette would not leave for Brown's Park without the dough he had feloniously acquired at Muddy Mischief Gap. But it was Charlotte who entered the barn first. Her agonized scream of horror came moments after Drew joined her.

The horrific sight of the blood-stained foreman pinned to the wooden stall, hanging there like a lump of butchered meat, was more than even he could bear. The woman turned away burying her head in his chest. He held her shuddering body close, stroking her head.

Much as he wanted to sooth her grief, this was no time for emotions to take control. Every minute lost here was one more for Sublette to make good his escape. Gently but firmly he extricated himself from the clinging embrace. 'Look after your ma, Chester. I need to get after the varmint that has done this.'

Though likewise distressed, the boy nodded his

152

understanding and pointed to a chestnut roan in one of the bays. 'Fleetfoot, over yonder has almost the same stamina as Tumbleweed. He'll see you right.'

Drew nodded his appreciation. 'I'll be back as soon as possible,' he whispered in the ear of the tearful woman.

'You be careful,' she sobbed looking him in the eye. 'I don't want you ending up another of that bastard's victims.' The unlikely blasphemy passed unnoticed. In the heat of the moment it seemed entirely appropriate.

Drew wiped a tear from her eye and kissed her on the cheek. 'It's a promise,' he murmured. Then pragmatism took over. Speed was now of the essence. And within moments he was mounted and heading off in the direction of Bridger.

CHAPTER SIXTEEN

CROSS OF RETRIBUTION

The first place Drew visited when he reach Bridger was the jail house. Without any preamble, he snapped out, 'Has Sublette been here?'

Coonskin was a mite taken aback by the deputy's sharp manner. 'No, he ain't, Deputy,' the turnkey replied somewhat tartly. 'But I saw him entering the courthouse about an hour since. And he looked in a mighty big hurry. Some'n going on here I should know about?'

'That devil-may-care all-action lawman Vince Sublette is nought but a thief and a murderer.' The rasping accusation hit the old jasper like a slap in the kisser. 'He's one of the brains behind the unexplained robberies around here and those missing deputies.'

'And who's the other guy behind all this mayhem? – Mayor Gillan I suppose.' The turnkey's sarcastic retort indicated he didn't believe a word of what he thought was a spurious charge. 'Where's your proof anyway?'

'You're way off'n the mark with Gillan. It was Farthing, that alleged upright citizen, who organized the robberies. And now he's dead, shot by Sublette. And I'm the only witness.' He shook his head in frustration. 'There ain't time for explanations. But I can prove my claim.' He immediately went into the cell block. 'You men should know that Farthing is dead and Sublette has skedaddled for Brown's Park with all the dough from the Muddy Mischief heist.'

'What you talking about?' Rufe Kegan blustered. 'We don't know anything about no heist. Ain't we been holed up in this dump waiting on the prison wagon?'

'I know what's been going on around here. And you lot are the fall guys. Sublette's made fools of you, and now he's gone, taking all the dough with him.'

'You're bluffing. He wouldn't leave us in the lurch like that,' Kegan remonstrated, grasping the cell bars. 'We're all partners.' But straightaway he knew that he had given the game away.

'You stupid jerk,' Braddock rasped. 'It was a trick to make us talk. And you went and fell for it.'

'No trick, boys.' Drew casually leaned against the wall ensuring he was out of reach of grasping paws. 'It was me that challenged the robbers at Muddy Mischief. And I was there when Sublette gunned

155

down his buddy the judge at Dead Man's Gate. Fat boy was running scared because of those deputies that were killed. My betting is the double-crosser is headed for Brown's Park. Right now.'

The outlaws were nervously looking at one another, unable to grasp what they were being told. Drew levered himself off the wall and fastened a caustic peeper on each of the prisoners in turn. 'And I'm figuring you guys know how that robbery and all the others were pulled off. But I need your evidence to deliver that critter to the hangman.'

'Why should we help you?' Bull Braddock piped up.

'I'm the guy who can speak up for you with the territorial law authorities. Seeing as how I'm a BAD agent. . . .' He slowly uncovered his badge of office. Revered by some and detested by others, it produced the desired effect. The divulgence certainly struck a chord with Rufe Kegan who swallowed hard. 'The Bureau will place a lot of weight on my evidence to reduce your sentence. But first I need to catch up with Sublette and bring him back, along with the money he's stolen.'

The outlaws were muttering among themselves, unsure how to react. 'I'll let you mull it over for five minutes. If'n I'm gonna run that skunk to ground before he skips the territory I need to hit the trail pronto. It's in your hands, boys. A full sentence with hard labour, or a short sentence in a softer pen. They tell me that Sweetwater is one bad place to spend any length of time.'

He then left the badly shaken crew to decide their fate. Coonskin had been listening in, and was mighty scared. Now he knew for sure how those robberies had taken place. And it was his weakness for the demon drink that had made them possible. He was more jittery than a Mexican jumping bean.

Drew said nothing, allowing the old trapper to sweat before re-entering the cell block. 'So what's it gonna be, fellas?'

As leader of the gang, it had been agreed that Kegan should spill the beans. He quickly outlined the devious scheme planned by the two principal blackguards. 'And can we trust you to keep your word and speak up for us?' All five of the outlaws uneasily eyed the self-confident BAD agent.

Drew smiled. He'd heard all he needed to. The twisted leer bore every trace of a pact having been reached. 'I'll sure do my best for you, boys,' he said leaving the block. 'You can depend on me.' He would relate the facts and let the outlaws confess their involvement at the trial, but in no way play down the lawless actions of these desperadoes. They would have to take their chances of having a lenient judge to decide their ultimate fate.

Out in the office, old Coonskin was all apologies. 'Jeepers, mister,' he exclaimed, 'I never realized I'd drunk that much. That darned gavel-basher took advantage of . . .' he gulped, barely able to admit the truth '. . . my weakness. The critter was all smiles and friendliness while nobbling the bottle he left me. I feel such a darned fool.' He couldn't look the lawman in the eye. 'There's only one way I can atone for my stupidity.'

Ten minutes later, with Fleetfoot beneath him, Drew was back on the trail of the ruthless exploiter of the much revered tin star. As a trapper, Coonskin knew every inch of the hill country stretching south to the border where Brown's Park was located. He was sure that Sublette would take the main trail, avoiding rough country and hoping to put more miles behind him. The guy had tapped his protruding snout meaningfully.

'But I know of a short cut that will bring you out ahead of the varmint.' The old guy's mind had been working overtime to arrive at this solution. 'I can point you in the right direction if'n you'll forget about my . . . erm . . . misjudgement. Is it a deal?'

Drew knew that he had little choice but to accept. It was an easy decision to make. He had no wish to embarrass the poor guy further. Time was fast slipping away, and with it his chances of catching the fugitive.

So here he was, following the instructions given by the wily turnkey. It was a surprisingly simple route to follow, with distinctive landmarks such as Table Rock, Tabernacle Butte, the Owl's Head and Eagle Peak to guide him. One after another the distinctive features were passed as the trail twisted between canyons and draws in a general southerly direction. Coonskin had a canny head on his shoulders, clearly cultivated over years of living in the outback. He had even promised that by keeping to a steady canter, the pursuer would cut the main trail at a meeting of four trails called

Buckboard Cross.

The tense journey had taken two days, most of it in the saddle. On reaching the Cross, there as promised stood the ruins of an abandoned buckboard, stark and rigid like the exposed ribs of a dead animal. The sight gave him much cause for celebration as he offered up a silent prayer of thanks to his benefactor. All he could hope for now was that he was ahead of his quarry.

Four hours passed, each one more frustrating than the last, until Drew became convinced he had missed his quarry. Then he saw it: a plume of dust that could only have been made by a lone rider pushing his mount hard. Drew settled himself behind the wagon, his rifle poking out as he sighted along the barrel. And this one had been specially zeroed and checked by the Bridger gunsmith. As the rider came closer, it was clear that it was indeed Vince Sublette.

A sharp call to halt saw the rider dragging back on the reins. 'Better surrender while you can, Vince,' Drew called out. 'This is the end of the line. There'll be no Brown's Park for you.'

Initially the outlaw was stunned that his deputy had by some miracle got ahead of him. But he quickly recovered his self-control, a growl of rage issuing from between gritted teeth. 'I don't know how you did it, fella, but I aim to be in the Park by sundown. And no meddling busybody is gonna stop me.'

He hauled out his own Winchester and jacked a round up the spout. 'Prepare to meet your maker.' Gripping the horse tightly with both knees, he dug in his spurs and lurched forward. Levering and letting rip he forced Drew to duck down. Bullets plucked at the dead wood trying to bring the same end to the concealed man. But Drew was well hidden and able to poke the rifle through a convenient gap. Holding his breath he took careful aim as the thundering attacker bore down on him.

All it needed was one shot to bring his adversary tumbling from the saddle. Sublette hit the ground with a crash. It had only been a glancing strike against the horse's flank, but it was enough to cause the animal to falter, unseating its rider. Before the downed man could recover his wits, Drew was on him. The hard stock of the rifle effectively rendered him *hors de combat*. Using his own lariat, the winner of the deadly contest soon had his prisoner trussed up tighter than a Thanksgiving turkey.

The next thing Sublette was aware of was being led back in the direction he had come. Drew was forced to gag his captive for most of the return journey to silence the cussing and threats of retaliation – although he made certain the silenced outlaw knew exactly how he had been thwarted and what the outcome was likely to be. The prisoner's red face bursting with suppressed anger caused the BAD boy great delight.

He also made sure to rub salt in the wound by gleefully informing the spurned suitor of his success in courting the lovely owner of the Lazy K. It was not a done deal yet, but he omitted that part from the detailed explanation. There was every hope that it would be in the none-too-distant future.